Happy New Year from Harl[...]ne resolution the editors of Presents like to keep is making time just for themselves by curling up with their favorite books and escaping into a world of glamour, passion and seduction! So why not try this for yourselves, and pick up a Harlequin Presents today?

We've got a great selection for you this month, with THE ROYAL HOUSE OF NIROLI series leading the way. In *Bride by Royal Appointment* by Raye Morgan, Adam must put aside his royal revenge to marry Elena. Then, favorite author Lynne Graham will start your New Year with a bang, with *The Desert Sheikh's Captive Wife*, the first part in her trilogy THE RICH, THE RUTHLESS AND THE REALLY HANDSOME. Jacqueline Baird brings you a brooding Italian seducing his ex-wife in *The Italian Billionaire's Ruthless Revenge*, while in *Bought for Her Baby* by Melanie Milburne, there's a gorgeous Greek claiming a mistress! *The Frenchman's Marriage Demand* by Chantelle Shaw has a sexy millionaire furious that Freya's claiming he has a child, and in *The Virgin's Wedding Night* by Sara Craven, an innocent woman has no choice but to turn to a smoldering Greek for a marriage of convenience. Lee Wilkinson brings you a tycoon holding the key to Sophia's precious secret in *The Padova Pearls,* and, finally, in *The Italian's Chosen Wife* by fantastic new author Kate Hewitt, Italy's most notorious tycoon chooses a waitress to be his bride!

Harlequin Presents®

ITALIAN HUSBANDS

They're tall, dark…and ready to marry!

If you love reading about our sensual Italian
men, don't delay—look out for the next story
in this great miniseries!

Available only from Harlequin Presents®!

Kate Hewitt

THE ITALIAN'S CHOSEN WIFE

ITALIAN HUSBANDS

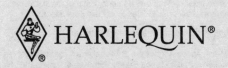

HARLEQUIN®

TORONTO • NEW YORK • LONDON
AMSTERDAM • PARIS • SYDNEY • HAMBURG
STOCKHOLM • ATHENS • TOKYO • MILAN • MADRID
PRAGUE • WARSAW • BUDAPEST • AUCKLAND

ISBN-13: 978-0-373-12698-9
ISBN-10:   0-373-12698-0

THE ITALIAN'S CHOSEN WIFE

First North American Publication 2008.

Copyright © 2007 by Kate Hewitt.

www.eHarlequin.com

Printed in U.S.A.

All about the author...
Kate Hewitt

KATE HEWITT discovered her first romance novel on a trip to England when she was thirteen, and she's continued to read them ever since. She wrote her first story at the age of five, simply because her older brother had written one and she thought she could do it, too. That story was one sentence long—fortunately, they've become a bit more detailed as she's grown older.

She studied drama in college and, shortly after graduation, moved to New York City to pursue a career in theater. This was derailed by something far better—meeting the man of her dreams, who also happened to be her older brother's childhood friend. Ten days after their wedding, they moved to England, where Kate worked a variety of different jobs—drama teacher, editorial assistant, youth worker, secretary and finally mother.

When her oldest daughter was a year old, Kate sold her first short story to a British magazine. Since then, she has sold many stories and serials, but writing romance fiction remains her first love—of course!

Besides writing, she enjoys reading, traveling and learning to knit—it's an ongoing process and she's made a lot of scarves. After living in England for six years, she now resides in Connecticut with her husband, her three young children—and possibly a dog one day.

Kate loves to hear from readers. You can contact her through her Web site, www.kate-hewitt.com.

To Cliff, for believing in me and showing it
in so many ways. —K.

PROLOGUE

'I WISH *that* was on the menu.'

Alessandro di Agnio's lips thinned in distaste at his companion's expression. He leaned back in his chair, his cool gaze flicking over the waitress chatting in Italian at the nearby table. Her hand rested on her hip, and he could hear the warm gurgle of her laughter from where he sat. There was, he noticed, a tomato sauce stain on her blouse. Her hair was falling from its pins, and she ran a careless hand through it.

His eyes narrowed. 'I believe we're here for the food.'

Next to him, his potential client Richard Harrison chuckled. 'Relax, di Agnio. It's just an expression.'

Alessandro smiled, his expression now calm, urbane, in place. He took a sip of iced water. 'She's quite pretty, in her own way. Now, to the business at hand…?' He raised his eyebrows, still smiling, although his eyes were cold and the expression on his face was at best remote.

Richard leaned back in his chair, his own expression that of a mouse intent on teasing a cat. His lower lip stuck out in a boyish pout. 'You know, I didn't come all the way to Spoleto just to talk to you. I thought we were going to have some fun.'

'Of course. You know what they say about all work and no play.' Alessandro shrugged lightly, although his eyes were still hard.

'Then how about a little play?' Richard asked, his tone turning petulant. 'I've heard so much about your playboy reputation. A few years ago there wasn't a tabloid in this country without your

picture splashed across its pages! Coming here, I was expecting
a little something more than lunch at a second-rate trattoria.'

Alessandro smiled again, this time a mere stretching of his
lips. He didn't need to be reminded of tabloids. Yet he also knew
how much Di Agnio Enterprises would benefit from Richard
Harrison's business.

'I didn't realise my reputation stretched so far,' he said after
a pause, his voice flat. 'Of course you need only choose your
pleasure. Dinner? Dancing?'

'Her.' Richard pointed to the waitress—still chatting,
Alessandro noticed, and obviously not an industrious worker. He
heard another peal of laughter, warm and inviting. She leaned
forward, hair tumbling into her face, one hand swiping it away
as she murmured provocatively. Everything about her told him
she was relaxed, carefree, available. Easy.

He'd known women like that. Knew what they wanted, what
they expected. Of him.

The customer she was talking to had to be seventy years old
at least. And he was eating it up. Probably wanted to eat *her*
up, as well.

'Her?' Alessandro repeated. Icy disbelief laced his words. 'I
don't pick women like sweets in a shop.' Not any more. He
injected a faint, dry note of humour into his voice as he added,
'I didn't think my reputation was quite that notorious.'

'I don't mean like *that*,' Richard said impatiently. He was
gazing at the waitress with the longing of a child for a toy—or,
as Alessandro had said, a sweet. A forbidden one, sticky and de-
lectable. 'She's a waitress. Why don't you hire her to wait on us
tonight? A quiet dinner for two, at your villa.' Richard's eyes lit
up lasciviously.

Alessandro eyed his companion with cold dislike. 'To wait on
us?' he repeated. 'And nothing else?'

Richard grinned. 'We could see what happens.'

Alessandro didn't bother to hide his disgust. His guest was
actually suggesting they hire the waitress as a virtual prostitute.
'I think not.'

'Why such a prude, di Agnio?' Richard taunted. 'From what

I hear, you've done that and worse.' He paused meaningfully. 'A lot worse.'

Alessandro did not dignify his companion's remark with a response. He knew his own past. He knew what people believed. He chose to ignore it, as he had ignored every telling, incredulous remark since he'd taken the reins of Di Agnio Enterprises two years ago.

'If it's pleasure you're seeking,' he said, with quiet, menacing derision, 'you'll find a wider range of amusements in town, not with some two-bit part-time whore.'

'You don't need to be crude.' Richard sipped his wine, his expression thoughtful as he gazed at the waitress. She'd finally cleared the table, dirty plates stacked on one tanned arm.

Still chatting, Alessandro noticed with scathing disdain. He watched her lips curl into a smile that promised all too much.

'She reminds me of home. I bet she's American.'

'Why don't you go talk to her, then?' Alessandro questioned silkily. 'I'm sure you don't need my intervention.'

'But I want it.' Richard's eyes met Alessandro's, watery blue clashing with midnight steel. 'And you need my business, di Agnio, so why don't you just humour me?'

A muscle ticked in Alessandro's jaw. He rested his hand flat on the table, resisting the desire to curl it into a fist. He would not be threatened—not by the potential of Harrison's business, not by the ghosts of his own past.

He was free. He was free of all that.

He smiled. 'You'll find I don't need your business quite as much as you think,' he said lightly. 'And perhaps you need mine a bit more than you'd like me to believe.'

Richard's expression hardened. Fear flickered in his eyes, and one limp, well-manicured hand bunched the tablecloth. 'Where did you hear that?'

'I like to stay informed.' Alessandro's smile widened, predatory, in control. Richard saw, and seemed to shrink a little. 'There's a dinner and dancing club on the Via Filetteria that will do very well for tonight.' Alessandro spoke firmly, as a parent to a child, and saw with satisfaction that Richard Harrison's momentary flare of rebellious authority had died out.

'I just liked her, that's all.'

Alessandro glanced again at the waitress. He could understand her appeal, on a basic level. She was pretty enough, and there was an aura about her that exuded—what? Warmth? Sexuality? Availability, perhaps?

A woman to be pleasured—used—once, and discarded.

If he did that. Which he did not.

Not any more.

Then she turned and caught his gaze. Her hair was piled untidily on top of her head, strands of indeterminate brown falling to frame her face. Nothing special, Alessandro decided dismissively, despite her youth and obvious sex appeal. She knew how to work a room, a man.

Then her eyes widened, her gaze fastened on his.

Her eyes were the golden-green of sunlight on an olive grove, iridescent, filled with promise. With hope. Her lips parted into a smile, tender in its uncertainty.

Alessandro felt his insides tighten. Something flared to life within him—something he'd suppressed, had thought banished for ever.

Need.

He turned back to Richard, who was oblivious to the silent yearning exchange. 'On second thoughts, I've changed my mind,' he said, in a voice that brooked no argument, no opposition. His fingers toyed with then tightened on the stem of his water glass. 'A quiet dinner at home will suit my needs.'

CHAPTER ONE

'MEGHAN, there's someone here to see you.'

Meghan Selby struggled against the knot in her apron strings and sighed tiredly.

'Please tell me it's not Paulo,' she said, as the other waitress, Carla, placed a stack of dirty plates on the counter.

'Who?'

'My landlord.'

Carla wrinkled her nose. 'What does he look like?'

'Short, fat, greasy-haired.' She suppressed a shudder.

'Why would he come here?' Carla asked, curiosity evident in her eyes, and Meghan shrugged evasively.

'Who knows? But I don't know many other people in this town.'

'Well, it's certainly not him.' Carla's efficient fingers went to work on the knot. 'This man is tall, built, wavy-haired and asking to see you.' She released the untangled strings and grinned. 'He's gorgeous, actually. Is there something—or someone—you're not telling me about?'

'I wish.' Meghan slipped off her apron with a quick, grateful smile. 'It's probably just someone who's lost his wallet.'

Carla raised her eyebrows. 'Why wouldn't he ask Angelo, then?'

She shrugged. The truth was, she'd no idea why a strange man would ask for her, and she didn't really want to know. She didn't want to attract attention from any men, strange or familiar. The sooner she dealt with the one waiting outside the better.

She'd been waitressing in Spoleto for six weeks, and she knew instinctively it was time to move on. She enjoyed Carla's friendship, and Angelo, who owned the trattoria, was like a doting uncle. She'd made a few friends in town, but she felt the inexorable need to shake the dust from her feet before the money ran out, before anyone got too close. Before her past caught up with her.

'I'll see you tomorrow?' Carla queried, and Meghan pretended not to hear. Best not to make any promises.

'I'd better go and see about my mystery man,' she joked, and Carla laughed.

'I can't wait to hear all about it.'

A quick glance in the bar's mirror revealed a stain on her shirt, and her hair, which had been in an almost sleek chignon this morning, was now a flyaway tangle.

'You look gorgeous, *cara*.' Angelo, sixty-three years old and full of spicy humour, grinned at her. 'Got a date?'

'Nope,' Meghan replied, trying for a breezy smile. She didn't plan on having any dates for a long time. She tucked a strand of hair behind her ear—not that it did much to help.

'See you tomorrow.'

She nodded, still making no promises, and went outside.

The man waiting under the red and white striped awning of Trattoria di Angelo was striking even from a distance. He wore a charcoal-grey suit, excellently cut, his hands thrust into the pockets of his trousers, stretching the cloth of his jacket against an impressive pair of shoulders.

He looked up as she approached, navy eyes clashing with hers. The sheer force of those eyes—the power, the *knowledge* in their midnight depths—made her take an involuntary step backwards even as her heart stumbled in beat.

She recognised him, of course, as the man who'd dined in the trattoria earlier. Someone important in business, or so Angelo's significant look had implied when he'd asked her to wait on them.

She remembered the way the man had looked at her earlier that afternoon, his eyes blazing into hers. Searing, branding.

Knowing.

As if he knew who she was. *What* she was.

That wasn't possible, Meghan reassured herself, and yet one look from beneath those dark, frowning brows told her this man had summed her up—and dismissed her—in a matter of seconds.

Opinions, impressions already formed, and they hadn't exchanged a word.

She straightened her shoulders, her expression hardening as a matter of instinct and self-preservation. She stopped a few feet from where he paced restlessly on the cobbled pavement.

'You wanted to see me?'

'Alessandro di Agnio,' he introduced himself brusquely, and thrust one hand out for her to shake.

Meghan inclined her head in introduction, resisting the impulse—the desire—to take his hand. Long, tapered fingers, strong, square nails. No, she didn't want to touch him. Didn't want to invite that particular temptation into her life.

'I don't think I know you,' she said, for he was still staring at her, eyes narrowed, mouth thinned in…what? Disapproval? Dislike? Disdain? Whatever it was, Meghan didn't like it.

He dropped his hand, smiling slightly in rueful acknowledgement of her rebuff.

'No, you don't. Not yet. But I hope you will very shortly.' His mouth curved in a small wry smile that flickered along her nerve-endings, skittered across her pulse. 'I wanted to hire your services for the evening.'

Meghan recoiled in spite of her best intentions to stay aloof. His words echoed in her brain. *Hire your services.* His meaning, the desire darkening his eyes, the faintly sneering curl of his lip, were plain enough.

She lifted her chin, summoned her strength. 'Services? I think you're talking to the wrong woman, *signore*.'

There was a moment of charged silence as he regarded her in obvious distaste. 'Perhaps I am. I need to hire a waitress for a private dinner party at my villa.' He raised an eyebrow, humour and contempt mingling in those dark, knowing eyes. 'Or were you thinking of some other kind of services?'

Humiliation burned colour in her cheeks. Her stomach felt as if it were coated in ice…or acid. Still Meghan glanced at him coolly, refusing to be unnerved. Condemned. 'A strange man asks to see me in the middle of the street—wants to hire my *services*— what am I supposed to think?'

'I can hardly put myself in your place, but I would imagine most women wouldn't immediately think they'd been mistaken for a whore.'

'Most women wouldn't appreciate being looked over like a piece of meat,' Meghan replied shortly. The word echoed in her numb brain. *Whore.*

A faint blush stained Alessandro di Agnio's sharp cheek-bones, and he gave a slight nod of acknowledgement. Meghan knew his type well enough to know there would be no apology forthcoming.

'I'm sorry,' he said, surprising her. 'You're a beautiful woman, and Italian men admire that. Some are more obvious than others. I promise you, I want to hire you as a waitress only, at my villa. It's a private dinner party for two.'

No doubt the business colleague from lunch, Meghan surmised. She'd seen the way his watery eyes had roved over her, the way his little mouth had pursed in greedy desire.

Yet she wasn't afraid of that man.

She was afraid of this one.

Afraid of his power, his effortless control, the way his eyes swept her from head to foot…the way her body reacted, tensing, tingling.

He had the face of an angel, Meghan thought, with those liquid eyes and sculpted lips. Not the innocent round-faced cherubs she'd seen in frescoes, but something elemental, beautiful in its power. His jaw was square, cheek-bones chiselled. A dangerous angel.

She shook her head. 'Why me?'

'I want a pretty girl as a waitress.' He shrugged, unapologetic. Unashamed. 'Someone to lighten the atmosphere, add a bit of flair. It's not an uncommon desire.'

Meghan cringed just a little bit at his words. A pretty girl. That was all she was, all she'd ever be. So little, so damning.

'Lighten the atmosphere?' she repeated, with a scornful note of incredulity. 'I'm not an entertainer.'

'Aren't you?' His eyes burned her from head to toe, and a slow smile stole over his features.

Meghan flushed angrily. He might not have said it in so many words, but she knew what he thought. Perhaps even what he expected. 'You don't know me, *signore*,' she said in a voice of restrained fury. '*You don't know me.*'

'No, I don't.' His eyes flicked coolly back up to her face. 'Not yet. So what will it be? I'll pay you double what you make at Angelo's.' There was an impatient edge to his voice. 'Triple. I'm sure you could use the money.' His dispassionate glance raked her again, taking in her worn white tee shirt with its tomato sauce stain, the black skirt that was cheap and shiny from wear.

Meghan refused to be embarrassed. She was a waitress; of course she was poor. Of course she could use the money.

And yet she didn't like the way Alessandro looked at her. As if he were buying goods, services, and cheap ones at that.

'Well?'

Meghan knew she should say no. Whatever Alessandro di Agnio said about hiring her as a waitress, she knew there were other expectations involved. A man didn't look at her like that if he just wanted her to serve food.

And yet Alessandro di Agnio hardly seemed like the kind of man who needed to purchase his pleasure.

Her stomach roiled with nerves; doubt wound tendrils around her heart. She didn't know what kind of man he was. She wasn't sure she wanted to find out.

She certainly didn't want to go to his villa alone, unprotected. Vulnerable.

Unless she could be stronger than that. Unless she could make it work to her advantage. Get through dinner, leave with euros in her pocket and a smile on her face.

Nothing changes the past.

No matter how far you run.

'One night,' Meghan clarified.

His lip curled. 'You want more?'

'Certainly not,' she snapped. 'I'm leaving Spoleto anyway.'

'Things not to your liking?'

Meghan's mouth hardened into an unforgiving line, a determination darkening her eyes. 'It's time to move on.'

'Then earn triple the last night you're here,' Alessandro suggested smoothly.

Meghan lifted her chin. Her pulse raced, blood rushed in her ears. 'Maybe I will.'

His eyes fastened on hers, and Meghan saw the hunger in them turning them opaque. She saw expectation, anticipation. Satisfaction. The deep, primal look of a conqueror regarding his spoils.

And she knew that, no matter what Alessandro said, he thought he was getting something more than a waitress for the night.

And was he?

No. For once she would prove who she was. What she was. And what she wasn't.

'Yes, I'll do it,' she said, her voice coming out strident. 'What time do you want me to come? And where?'

'Villa Tre Querce. It's five kilometres outside of town. I'll send a car.'

'No.' She didn't want his car showing up at the grotty hostel she currently called home, and she didn't want to take anything else from Alessandro di Agnio. 'I'll take the bus.'

'The buses don't go to Tre Querce,' Alessandro informed her shortly. 'I have a car and a driver. Give me your address, and I'll send him to fetch you at seven o'clock. We'll dine at eight.'

'That doesn't give me much time,' Meghan protested. 'It must be six o'clock now.' Already there was a slight chill in the spring air, descending damply from the mountains, rolling in on a fine mist.

'All the more reason for me to send the car,' Alessandro countered, and his tone brooked no opposition. 'Tell me your address.'

Meghan shrugged. Let him see where she lived. It was dire, she knew that, but who cared?

She didn't. He certainly didn't.

'It's the Arbus Hostel on the west side of town,' she informed him coolly. 'On the Via Campelo.'

His mouth tightened in disapproval. 'I don't know it.'

'You wouldn't.'

'My driver will be there at seven.' He paused, his gaze flicking the length of her, taking in, no doubt, her mussed hair and stained shirt.

'You have something to wear?'

Her eyebrows lifted in challenge. 'I'm waitressing, remember? I think I have something suitable.'

'This isn't the trattoria,' Alessandro warned her. 'I expect you to dress…and behave…appropriately.'

The warning stung. 'It's a little late now for second thoughts, isn't it?' Meghan said, her smile cautious. 'You've already hired me.' Her voice turned ragged as she added, 'I'm not going to show up in nothing but high heels and a frilly apron, even if that's what you actually want—'

'Stop it.' Alessandro's voice cut across her. 'I've told you what this position entails—waitressing and nothing more. Do you not trust me?'

Meghan dared herself to meet his eyes, to feel the force of their magnetic onslaught. Trust? What a joke. She barely knew him, and even if she did, the only trust she had was in herself, in her ability to protect herself. 'Is there any reason,' she asked quietly, 'why I *should* trust you?'

Alessandro gazed at her in silent consideration. He shrugged and looked away. 'No,' he said after a moment, his voice flat and expressionless, 'there isn't.'

Meghan sagged slightly. Of course there wasn't. She was walking into the lion's den, and she wasn't even armed. All she had was her dignity and her determination to prove herself, and right now they didn't count for much.

'I'll see you, then,' she said after a moment, thankful her voice was steady. She began to turn away, only to have Alessandro reach out. He put his hand on her arm, his fingers wrapping around her wrist, pulling her towards him.

Meghan stiffened with shock and a little fear. Shock at his touching her, the simple, possessive way he drew her to him. Thoughtlessly, and yet with care. As if already he expected something from her, deserved something from her.

The fear was at her own reaction. She didn't resist. She let him pull her, her legs moved woodenly, helplessly, closer. Her pulse kicked into high gear with the simple touch of those fingers on her wrist, holding her. Gently.

He kept holding onto her, a slight smile playing about his mouth, his eyes raking in her appearance, their gaze a caress...and an assessment.

'I don't even know your name.'

Her lips opened soundlessly as her mind spun. 'Meghan.'

He nodded. He let go of her wrist, smiling as she pulled her arm protectively inwards. 'I'll see you at seven.'

Meghan's legs trembled as she watched him walk away. She shook her head, resisting the urge to wrap her arms more tightly around herself. Had she really agreed to waitress? *Why?* It should have been so easy to walk away.

Yet it wasn't, and she hadn't.

She couldn't escape her past, she reflected bleakly. The exchange with Alessandro di Agnio reminded her of that. If anything happened tonight it would be nothing more than she deserved.

CHAPTER TWO

MEGHAN hurried through the darkening streets of Spoleto towards the Via Campelo and the hostel she'd been calling home.

Not a very pleasant home at that, with its tiny dark bedrooms, dripping ceilings and grimy sheets. She'd seen worse on her travels, but Paulo, the proprietor, was a particularly unpleasant landlord.

Meghan had seen him for what he was right away. First it had just been leering grins and wandering eyes, soon followed by coarser remarks and wandering hands.

She'd bought a padlock for her door, and more than once she'd woken up to hear the stealthy, futile turning of the door handle, weak with relief that she was at least that safe.

Now she tried to avoid him altogether. Still, it was another reason to leave Spoleto. With the money earned from waitressing for di Agnio she could buy a train ticket to her next destination…wherever that was.

'*Ciao, bellissima.*' Paulo leaned over the front desk as Meghan slipped in the door. His white undershirt sported large patches of dried sweat, and his mouth curled in a knowing grin, revealing tobacco-stained teeth.

Meghan didn't bother to answer. She slipped by before he could reach one hand out to squeeze or pat, and hurried to her room, fastening the padlock.

There was no time for a shower, so she just splashed water on her face and arms from the tiny cracked sink in the corner of the room.

She threw her dirty clothes in the corner and pulled on a fresh white shirt and simple black skirt—her waitressing uniform. She hadn't brought much with her when she'd left home. It had all been so quick in the end.

Dressed and ready, she sank onto the bed, the broken springs creaking in protest. Her momentary burst of energy spent, she felt weak. Limp. Unreal.

The conversation with Alessandro di Agnio played in her mind, forever on pause and rewind.

Why had she agreed? she asked herself again, and couldn't come up with a satisfactory answer. At least not one she was willing to face.

In the last six months of travelling through Europe, she'd become a professional at deflecting comments, invitations, innuendoes. A woman on her own was considered fair game, easy prey by many, and Meghan already knew of her own damning allure.

So why hadn't she just said no to Alessandro di Agnio? It would have been easy. It would have been safer to have just walked away.

Because he's different.

The thought was ludicrous, laughable. Stupid.

He'd summed her up quickly enough—easy American, slutty waitress. He wasn't going to change his mind.

She was the one who would prove she was different. *This time.*

'I won't see him again after tonight,' Meghan muttered, and it was both thanksgiving and supplication.

He certainly wasn't expecting to see *her* again, she reflected with a wry bitterness. One night only, limited engagement.

She pulled her hair back into a sleek ponytail, her only concession to vanity a bit of face powder and lipgloss. The last thing she wanted was for di Agnio to think she was tarting herself up.

She locked her room and went in search of Paulo.

'I'll have my deposit back, please. I'm leaving tomorrow.'

Paulo looked at her with calculating lasciviousness. 'I don't remember you putting down a deposit. I said you didn't have to, because you were so pretty.'

Meghan gritted her teeth. 'Nice try, Paulo. I have the receipt.

Two weeks' stay in this hovel. That will cover last week's rent, and the rest I want back. Now.'

His expression hardened. 'Don't talk mean to me, *principessa*. I know what you are.'

'I'm a waitress,' Meghan snapped, her already frayed temper now reaching breaking point. She might have been unnerved by Alessandro di Agnio, but she certainly wouldn't be so shaken by this piece of wheedling slime.

'You need the money?' His eyebrows rose. 'You're in trouble, perhaps?'

'No, and no,' Meghan retorted. 'But that doesn't stop me from wanting what's mine.'

'Maybe *I* want what's mine.' There was a thread of dangerous need in Paulo's voice, and Meghan's scalp prickled in alarm. She took a step away, but not fast enough.

Paulo grabbed her arm and pulled her to him. Meghan slammed against his soft belly with a suppressed grunt, his hands tight on her wrists, pinning her against him.

'One kiss.'

She could smell his stale smoky breath, his old sweat. She could smell his lust, and everything in her recoiled.

'Get off me—' Meghan tried to push herself away, but Paulo only held her tighter.

'One kiss, *bella*, that's all. And then you can have your money.'

'Go to hell!' Meghan spat raggedly. 'I won't give you anything—'

'You've been wanting it.' Paulo's face had turned angry even as his eyes were bright with desire. Meghan wanted to retch. 'I've seen you—the looks you give me—'

She closed her eyes, swallowed bile. 'You're fooling yourself, Paulo, and I can call the police—'

'But you haven't, have you?' he said with soft menace. His lips, moist and slimy, were inches from hers. 'I've wondered about you, *bella*. What are you trying to hide? Why don't you leave? You could, you know. There are other hostels in Spoleto.' He shook his head slowly. 'But you never did leave...so that must mean you want it.'

'You're wrong.' Meghan's voice shook. Her body shook. She felt weak and helpless, and the realisation angered her. She would not be a victim again. She would not allow someone as pathetic and disgusting as Paulo to control her.

Except she couldn't prevent him.

He was too strong, and every time she struggled the hands grasping both her wrists, forcing her to press up against him, tightened.

'Let me go,' she cried desperately, and Paulo's eyes glittered.

'I want to hear you beg.'

'You will be the one begging. To the police.' The voice from the doorway was like the crack of a pistol. Paulo's grip slackened, and Meghan stumbled away, a trembling sob escaping from her before she could prevent it.

Alessandro stood in the doorway, his face white with rage. His whole body was tensed, coiled, ready to spring. He stared at Paulo with glittering eyes.

'I'm calling the police.'

'You can't prove anything,' Paulo said sullenly, but he looked nervous.

'You'll find,' Alessandro said, in a voice that was deadly in its quiet calm, 'that I can prove whatever I want. When the *carabiniere* arrive they will only need my word to see you rot in jail.'

'She wanted it—' Paulo began, but Alessandro cut him off with one sharply raised hand. Every movement was efficient, precise. Taut with suppressed emotion.

'Do not tell me what any woman wants. You should not presume to know.' He dropped his hand. 'Do you know who I am?'

Paulo's eyes shifted nervously, speculatively, to Meghan. 'No…'

'I am Alessandro di Agnio. This hostel will be shut down by morning.'

Paulo's face paled and his mouth dropped open. 'Di Agnio…but you can't do that! There are people staying here—I own it—'

Alessandro's face was implacable. 'It will be shut.' He snapped open his mobile phone. 'Now I am calling the police.'

'Signor di Agnio—' Meghan's voice came out in a choked whisper. She was still reeling from shock, her senses struggling to catch up. She dragged a breath into her lungs, ran a hand through her mussed hair. 'Please don't involve the police.'

Alessandro turned to look at her sharply. 'What? Are you in trouble with the police?'

Meghan almost laughed at his assumption. 'No, I'm not. I just don't want them involved—the time and hassle it will cause. There will be a report to give, no matter what your word means in Spoleto.'

He searched her face, as if looking for an answer to an unspoken question. Meghan said nothing.

'Please, let's just go.'

The silence was taut as Alessandro gazed at her. Paulo watched them from behind his desk, his expression one of a trapped mouse, scenting both freedom and danger.

Alessandro snapped his mobile shut. He didn't even glance at Paulo as he said, 'The hostel will close tonight. For good. I do not want to see you in Spoleto again.'

He walked out, and Meghan had no choice but to follow.

Outside his car idled at the kerb. It was not, as Meghan had half-expected, a sleek sports car, the embodiment of most Italian males' fantasies. It was instead a luxury executive model. Alessandro opened the door and stood aside for her to get into the front passenger seat. Every movement spoke of barely curbed impatience.

Meghan stared at him with wide eyes, suddenly realising the enormity of his presence. 'I thought you were going to send a driver.'

'I decided to come myself instead.'

Somehow this didn't surprise her. Alessandro di Agnio was a man who was in control. Always. Wordlessly she slipped inside.

The car was cool and the leather seat soft and inviting. Meghan leaned her head against the seat and closed her eyes. She didn't want to talk, and to her surprise and relief Alessandro remained silent as he got in and pulled away from the kerb, navigating Spoleto's evening traffic with superb confidence.

Meghan opened her eyes and stared blindly at the traffic— cars and mopeds weaving around each other on the narrow cobbled streets. As they broke free from the city and its traffic the Umbrian hills, cloaked in purple twilight, spread out before them, and the sounds of urban life were replaced by the quietness of meadow and field.

She snuck a peek at Alessandro's profile. The sharp, clean line of his tensed jaw, his powerful shoulders still encased in the charcoal-grey suit, his hands easily gripping the steering wheel— all radiated power. Confidence. Control.

Over her.

No. She couldn't let that happen.

Yet she felt as if the whole situation had started slipping away from her from the moment Alessandro had walked into the hostel.

No, she realised with a sigh, from the moment he'd asked her to waitress.

If she'd ever thought she was in control of this situation, of *him*, she'd been massively deluded.

She wasn't in control of anything—least of all her own spinning emotions.

Alessandro slotted her a sideways look out of steel-blue eyes, his lips tightening as his gaze swept over her.

'Are you all right?' he asked, and Meghan jerked back in surprise. 'What?'

Alessandro gestured to her wrist. A purple bruise was already starting to blossom on the tender skin. Meghan glanced at it and shrugged.

'I'm fine. I should have known Paulo would try something. I suppose I thought he was too much of a coward to live up to his filthy talk—'

'Why do you stay there?' Alessandro asked abruptly. 'There are plenty of hostels in Spoleto. Inexpensive hotels. You don't need to endure his filth.'

Meghan shrugged again. 'It was cheap and convenient,' she said, staring out of the window.

'Cheap I can believe. I'm surprised the building wasn't condemned. Convenient? No. What is convenient about being molested? Raped?'

'I wasn't raped.'

'You could've been.'

'Oh, am I supposed to thank you now?' Meghan asked, her voice sharp with sarcasm. 'I'm sorry, but I don't do the whole damsel in distress routine.'

'I've realised that.' The wry humour edging his voice took the wind straight out of her sails. Meghan sagged back against the seat.

'I'm sorry.'

'I'm not. I'm glad I was there in time.'

Meghan touched a finger to the bruise on her wrist. 'So am I,' she admitted quietly.

Alessandro watched her, his expression forbiddingly grim. 'At least no other women will suffer Paulo in this city,' he murmured, almost to himself, and Meghan lurched upright.

'Do you mean you were serious when you said you were shutting down the hostel?'

Alessandro looked affronted. 'Of course I was. Did you think I was bluffing?'

Definitely not, she conceded silently. 'But you can't just do that, can you? He said he owned the building.'

'He was lying. It's owned by a local businessman. I checked on it before I arrived.'

Of course, Meghan thought. In control. Again. 'If you don't own it, how can you make him close it down?' she pressed and Alessandro shrugged impatiently.

'Since you're American, you don't realise what the di Agnio name means in Italy—especially in Umbria.'

'You're powerful,' Meghan surmised, and he chuckled dryly.

'Most women find that attractive.'

'I don't.' She looked away. 'At least not when I'm on the wrong side of it.'

He glanced at her, curious. 'Do you think you are now?'

Was she? It was a question Meghan didn't want to ask herself. Certainly didn't want to answer. 'The thing about power,' she said after a moment, her voice brittle, 'is that it can easily be abused.'

'Agreed.' Alessandro's voice was terse. 'As in the case with

Paulo, don't you think?' he continued after a moment. 'At least you don't have to endure his attentions any more.'

'Then where am I supposed to sleep?'

'I can find you another hotel. Or you could sleep at my villa.'

Meghan reared back at his blatant offer. 'Thanks for the offer, but no thanks,' she replied sharply. 'I'd rather stay with Paulo.'

'Don't be absurd!'

'Don't think you can control me,' she fired back, fury starting to boil. Anger felt good. Clean.

'Control? Is that what you think this is about? I was protecting you back there!'

'I don't need protecting.'

He raised one eyebrow in scathing contempt. 'Really? It didn't look like it from where I was standing.'

Meghan gritted her teeth. 'I can handle Paulo.'

'You were obviously handling him when I came in,' Alessandro slung back at her. He shook his head in incredulous derision. 'Do you honestly think you could have controlled him?'

'I…' Meghan trailed off. *More than I can control you.*

The frightening thing was, she realised, she couldn't have controlled Paulo. She could have been—perhaps *would* have been—raped.

She bent over, suddenly feeling nauseous, the events of the evening catching up to her consciousness with sickening speed. 'I think I'm going to throw up.'

In one fluid movement Alessandro pulled the car over onto a stretch of grass and flung open his door. He went around to Meghan's door and yanked it open, ushering her out with one arm around her shoulders.

Meghan pushed away from him and stumbled into the grass where she retched helplessly. She'd never felt so low, so utterly humiliated, and that was saying something.

That was saying quite a lot.

She stood up, wiping her mouth, her hair falling about her face, while Alessandro watched impassively. He handed her a starched white linen handkerchief, and Meghan dabbed at her lips uselessly. She didn't want to sully it.

'It's to be used,' he said, his voice tart, and Meghan managed a weak smile.

'Sorry.'

'I'm the one who should be sorry. I should have remembered how shock can be delayed. Here.' He handed her a bottle of water and Meghan opened it, drinking gratefully.

'Thank you.'

'Are you ready?' he asked after a moment, and Meghan was suddenly aware of how dark it was. A car hadn't passed them since he'd pulled over, and nothing but meadows and clusters of elm trees surrounded them, the hills no more than shadowed mounds in the distance.

She could hear the whisper of the wind through the grass and the bare branches of the trees. She could hear her own breathing. They were very much alone.

'Yes, I'm ready.'

Alessandro opened the door for her, and Meghan slipped inside.

'I'm sorry about that,' she said again, once they were on the road, and Alessandro shrugged.

'Don't apologise.'

The car climbed higher into the Umbrian hills, and they spent the rest of the short drive in silence. Soon a high stone wall appeared, running parallel to the road.

Alessandro swung the car through an opened pair of ornate iron gates, and then up a long, twisting drive, the hills steep on either side.

Automated outdoor lights flashed on as the car approached the portico, and Meghan glimpsed a long, rambling villa of mellow stone and terracotta roof tiles. Several large pots lined the entrance, spilling a riot of begonias onto the tiled steps.

Alessandro stopped the engine and went around to open Meghan's door. She stepped out with murmured thanks. She smelled the fresh tang of pine, and the air was sharper, colder. She wrapped her arms around herself.

The front door opened, and a stout woman with a shiny black bun of hair, a spotless apron and a forbidding expression stood there. Meghan quailed under her heavy-browed, frowning gaze.

'Meghan, this is Ana,' Alessandro said, 'the housekeeper and guardian of Tre Querce.'

He spoke rapid Italian to Ana, too fast for Meghan's basic grasp of the language, and the woman gave an obviously disgruntled response.

'Ana will show you to a room,' he continued in English. 'You can freshen up and meet me in the lounge for dinner.'

Meghan turned to look at him in surprise. It almost sounded as if she were a guest rather than a waitress. 'Shouldn't I be in the kitchen?' she suggested hesitantly, and Alessandro gave her a knowing look.

'You are not the cook.'

'I'm a waitress,' she threw back at him, and his smile was far too understanding.

'Yes. I know. So you've told me.'

With jerky, unnatural steps Meghan followed Ana through a cool tiled hallway and up a wide staircase, her hand clutching the smooth wrought-iron banister.

Silently Ana led her down the upstairs hall, passing a row of closed doors, before ushering her into a bedroom spare and clean in its elemental luxury.

A large double bed dominated the room, the duvet and pillows encased in pure white linen. An oak dresser with iron fixtures stood against the wall, a strip of mirror above.

Disapproval radiated from every stiff line of the older woman, from her thinly pressed lips to the tightly clasped hands at her ample waist. Meghan couldn't blame her. What did she think she was? How had Alessandro explained her presence?

Why was she here?

Ana left without a word, and Meghan sank down on the bed, enjoying the softness, relieved to be alone even though her nerves felt as if they were jangling and jumping throughout her taut body.

Why was she here?

She looked in the mirror. Her hair had come undone, her face was pale and tense, her eyes as wide and frightened as a doe's.

Why was she here?

It wasn't for the money. She could have left Spoleto without it, Meghan acknowledged. Admittedly, it would come in handy, but still…

She didn't need it. Didn't even want it, perhaps.

She owed nothing to Alessandro di Agnio, nothing to anyone.

Yet she'd agreed. Willingly.

What did that make her? Meghan wondered. To agree to come to a strange man's house, despite the desire in his eyes, the assessment of his gaze, the innuendo in his tone.

He knew what she was.

Everyone knows what you are.

The voices from her past clamoured inside her head—a knowing hiss, a contemptuous snarl.

Had she come here to prove Alessandro di Agnio wrong… or right?

Or to prove something to herself? And to Stephen.

She stood up, filled with a sudden restless energy, and moved to the French doors that looked out on the villa's gardens. She saw a swimming pool set in resplendent grounds, closed now, and beyond that terraced gardens, shadowed and bare.

Meghan shivered. The night air in the mountains was cool, and her simple white shirt didn't give her much warmth or protection. She took in a shaky breath and set about repairing herself.

A few minutes later, her hair neat and her face clean, she stepped outside. The villa was quiet. She couldn't hear the murmur of voices or the clank of pans from the kitchen. Nothing.

Carefully she walked down the front stairs. A single light flickered in the foyer, and a pair of double doors had been left slightly open, leading to what looked like the lounge.

Meghan's heart thudded in fresh anxiety and she wiped her palms along the sides of the skirt.

She supposed she should go in there, search out Alessandro and his weasely friend. Do what she was being paid to do. Pass out *hors d'oeuvres*. Make conversation, smile. Flirt.

Except, quite suddenly, she couldn't. The thought made her ill; she was sickened by the very fact that Alessandro had asked and she'd agreed.

She couldn't do this.

She *was* doing this.

She shook her head, biting her lips, and half slunk down the hallway in search of the kitchen.

Ana looked up in frowning surprise as Meghan entered the spacious room. Gleaming chrome appliances and granite worktops gave way to a breakfast nook and more French doors that led out to the terrace and swimming pool. Although it was in darkness, Meghan could imagine the stunning view of hills Tre Querce possessed.

'I'm here to help,' she began awkwardly in Italian. 'I mean...to serve. You know?'

Ana stared at her. A pot bubbled on the stove, emitting a wonderful spicy scent. A green salad was in the process of being made on the worktop, next to fat red tomatoes and yellow peppers in a basket.

'Signor di Agnio doesn't want you here,' Ana said after a moment, choosing her words with care. 'He wants you in the lounge. Now.'

Meghan shook her head. Her nerves were taut as wire, threatening to snap. She couldn't face it...them.

'Perhaps,' she finally said, speaking slowly as she searched for the right words. 'But I came here to serve the food, and this is where the food is.'

'No.' Ana shook her head.

Meghan clenched her fists at her sides but kept her smile in place. 'Why don't I just put an apron on?' she suggested, and, spying one hanging on a hook by the door, slipped it on before Ana could protest.

The housekeeper shrugged, and turned away with a grunt.

Meghan scanned the worktop, wishing she could make herself useful. She wondered about the men waiting for her. What did they really expect? Would Alessandro come and find her?

She shivered. It was stupid to have come here, to have thought she could exorcise her personal demons by seeing this little arrangement through. She didn't have the strength, the power.

The control.

All she wanted to do now was run away. Hide. But where?

She suddenly appreciated how isolated Villa Tre Querce was, how isolated *she* was.

How alone.

Vulnerable.

'I thought you'd be hiding in here.'

She turned to see Alessandro standing in the kitchen doorway, one shoulder leaning against the frame. He'd changed out of his suit and now wore a casual white button-down shirt, open at the neck to expose the tanned column of his throat. He wore faded jeans with a leather belt, casual yet expensive, and fitting him far too wonderfully.

It was not, Meghan thought, an outfit a man wore to a business dinner. He looked too relaxed, too comfortable in his own skin for her liking. He looked ready to be entertained, amused, enjoyed.

She wanted business suits, papers and briefcases, laptops and mobiles. A business dinner, with both men too involved in their work to spare her a glance.

Except that was not how it was going to be…how Alessandro would let it be. She could tell that right now, in the way his lips curled upwards in a predatory smile, his eyes taking in her appearance, resting on her face with a flare of hunger, desire.

She was not making that up, she knew, nor the answering flicker in her own core.

She swallowed. 'Where else would I be? And I'm not hiding.'

'Of course not.' Humour lurked in those steely eyes, in the twitching of his moulded lips. He took a step into the kitchen. 'I thought I told you to meet me in the lounge.'

'Is your dinner companion in there?' She hated the fact that her voice wavered. 'Has he arrived already?'

'You'll see.' He twitched the apron from around her neck, balling it in his fist before tossing it aside. 'You don't need that.'

One more piece of her armour taken away. One more layer stripped bare.

'I didn't want to get my uniform dirty.'

He raised one eyebrow. 'Uniform?' he asked with obvious scepticism, before turning to leave the kitchen, clearly expecting her to follow. And, wordlessly, she did.

She followed him to the lounge, its double doors opening to a room scattered with comfortable sofas upholstered in varying shades of cream. The few pieces of artwork on the walls were vivid splashes of colour, still-lifes of flowers, scenes of Umbria in bold strokes, that made Meghan pause to admire their sheer vivacity.

Then she looked around. The room was empty.

'Where is your guest…?' she began, but something in Alessandro's satisfied look as he stood in the doorway made the question die on her lips. She had a bad feeling about this.

'*You* are my guest, Meghan,' he said softly. 'There is no one else.'

CHAPTER THREE

'No.' MEGHAN said the first word that came to mind, desperately wanting it to be true. 'No, no, no.'

'Yes.' Alessandro smiled. He seemed pleased. Far too pleased. As if he'd given her a gift, a pleasant surprise. A *treat*.

'You hired me to be a waitress,' Meghan pointed out in what she hoped was a reasonable tone. 'For a dinner party. That's why I'm here.'

'I hired you,' he agreed, 'but, as you remember, it was for a quiet dinner for two. There are two of us in this room right now.'

His words drenched her in icy shock. Meghan stared incredulously. 'You never even intended for someone else to come? What about the man you ate lunch with?'

Alessandro's expression hardened. 'He has other plans for the evening. He is a business acquaintance, nothing more.'

'And what am I?' Her voice rose shrilly, and she pressed a fist to her lips. She moved around the room restlessly, seeking escape, but there was none. She didn't have a car. She didn't even know where the villa was. She had no place to go in Spoleto. And Alessandro was blocking the door.

She'd walked straight into a trap. She'd agreed to it willingly. Who wouldn't think she deserved this, that she wanted this? Disgust roiled through her, washed over in sickening waves. Terror followed on its heels. She closed her eyes, struggling for composure. Control.

She opened them, saw Alessandro regarding her with a

mixture of curiosity and compassion. She took a deep, shuddering breath. There was always Ana in the kitchen. She could handle this. She had to handle this.

'Whatever you thought about me, it's wrong. I don't want to be here. I don't want to have dinner with you. Take me back to Spoleto now or I'll press charges.'

Alessandro raised his eyebrows, taking in her words with a thoughtful nod. 'You're scared,' he said after a moment.

Meghan laughed shrilly. 'Of course I'm scared! A strange man—a powerful man—has trapped me in his house, alone! Under false pretences! Now, let me go.'

He continued watching her, his expression assessing but not without compassion. Meghan didn't care. Couldn't think. She paced the room, caged and desperate.

'Why weren't you frightened,' he asked after a moment, 'when you believed I'd hired you to serve my lunch guest and me? Then there would have been two men here with you. Shouldn't that have been twice as alarming?'

Meghan whirled around and glared at him, fear replaced momentarily by anger. 'It was a *business* arrangement.'

He shrugged. 'Then consider this such an arrangement as well. I'll pay you the same rates. I just want to have dinner with you.'

'I don't want to be paid!' she snapped. 'I'm not a whore!'

Alessandro stilled, his expression chilling. 'I don't remember calling you that.'

She closed her eyes, pressed a hand to her chest as if she could still the frantic racing of her heart. 'If you wanted to have dinner with me,' she said after a few seconds of silence, her breathing ragged, uneven, 'then there are more normal ways to have gone about it. You could have asked me straight out. It's called a date.'

'Admittedly I've used unconventional means.' He shrugged, unperturbed. 'I had to.'

'Oh? And why is that?'

'I'm a powerful man, Meghan. You remember that power can be abused? It works both ways.' He smiled softly. 'Picture this. A man is charmed by a pretty young waitress when he sees her in a restaurant. He likes her smile, and the way her eyes remind him of sunlight. He wants to get to know her better, but he also understands that his position and wealth either frighten women off or attract the wrong kind. So he makes up a little pretence to bring this woman he desires to his house. Nothing far-fetched, nothing sordid. And when she arrives, he intends to surprise her with a quiet, romantic dinner. A chance to know her, and for her to know him. And then he drives her home.'

Meghan stared at him, arrested. Her lips parted, but no words came out. Her mind whirled, thoughts twisting away before she could snatch them, drag them to clarity. 'It wasn't like that.'

'Wasn't it?' Alessandro's quiet, sad little smile made her heart ache with regret and wonder.

It wasn't like that.

She shook her head. She couldn't believe. Couldn't let herself. 'You can romance it up all you want now, because you think I want to hear those silly pretty words. But you as good as admitted what you really want…what you really think of me. We both know that.'

'What I want to know,' Alessandro said softly, 'is why you think so little of yourself.'

'I don't,' Meghan snapped—a matter of instinct, yet her words sounded hollow. She turned away. 'Why can't you just take me home?'

'Because I don't want to.' Alessandro sat in an armchair, ivory silk striped with gold, his legs elegantly crossed, his body relaxed. 'Where do you come from?' he asked pleasantly. 'Why have you been travelling around Europe? Waitressing to pay your way, I presume?'

'Stop it.' She shook her head. 'This is a farce. I'm not sitting here talking with you, discussing my life with you.'

'It would perhaps make things more pleasant.'

'I don't *want* things to be pleasant,' she snapped. 'I want to leave here. Now.'

'Then answer my questions. Ask some of your own. It's called making conversation, you know.'

'All right.' She dropped her hands, took a deep breath. 'Here's a question…Alessandro. If I have dinner with you, will you drive me back to Spoleto afterwards?'

'If that's what you want.' The implication was obvious. Dinner would be enough to make her change her mind. He smiled; it felt like a caress. 'I like the way you say my name.'

Meghan stared at him, watched as the heat in his eyes flared, turning them from steely-blue to indigo, and she wondered helplessly, hopelessly, if dinner would indeed be enough.

'You do not need to be frightened,' Alessandro said quietly. 'That was never my intention. You can trust me.'

'You told me not to,' Meghan snapped, and Alessandro's expression hardened for a moment.

'I told you there was no reason to. Now there is.'

'Oh, and what is that?'

He smiled, although his eyes remained flinty. 'Because I said so.'

She opened her mouth to utter some scathing reply, the words not yet formed in her head, but then something left her. Her energy, perhaps, or at least her self-righteousness. Her ability to continue a verbal battle with this impossible iron-willed man. And her fear.

She sank onto a cream leather sofa and leaned her head against its soft back. 'You speak English very well,' she said after a moment.

'Thank you. I should. I spent most of my boyhood in England.'

'Why?'

'I went to boarding school at seven, in Winchester,' he explained. 'All of my siblings did.'

'You have brothers and sisters?'

'One sister.' He opened his mouth to speak, and then shut it abruptly. Meghan almost asked what he'd been going to say, but the shuttered look in his eyes made her realise that topic was now off limits. All of his siblings had gone to boarding school, yet he only had one sister? Something didn't make sense.

'Who are the di Agnios, anyway?' she asked. 'Something big, obviously, but what do you do?' She sat up straight, the thought of the Mafia suddenly shooting through her. Surely not…

'We're entrepreneurs.' The rich laughter lacing his words showed he knew exactly where her train of thought had led her.

'Primarily jewellery, but we've branched into property, finance—a bit of everything really.'

'Di Agnio…' With a jolt Meghan remembered passing boutiques of that name, shops with locked doors and luxurious velvet cases in their display windows. As far as jewellery went, it was strictly top-shelf. 'It's a family business?'

'Yes. I am the CEO.'

Well. She sat back again, realising sickly the kind of life he must lead—so different from hers. It would be nice, to have that kind of wealth, power, control. Safety.

She took a deep breath, let it out. 'All right, then. Let's have dinner.'

Alessandro grinned, and the effect was quite devastating. Meghan drew in a shaky uneven breath at the sight of him, the harsh lines of his face relaxed into laughter, the whiteness of his smile contrasting with his tanned skin and navy eyes, now glinting with humour.

When Alessandro di Agnio frowned he was forbidding. In repose he was handsome, even beautiful. But when he smiled Meghan wanted to walk straight into his arms.

And that was a place she could not go.

'Then you take me home,' she added, and he nodded.

'Of course. If you wish.'

'I will wish it,' Meghan snapped, and he merely chuckled.

Damn him. Damn his arrogance, and damn him for being right. Already she felt herself wondering, weakening.

Wanting.

A smile played about his mouth as he held out his hand. 'Shall we?'

She still had things to prove. She would still walk away with her dignity, her pride, her heart.

Her heart? The last thought, slipping treacherously through her numb brain, made Meghan almost gasp in surprise.

There was no way her heart was involved with this man.

'All right,' she agreed tonelessly.

She walked past him, towards the kitchen, but Alessandro pulled her back gently, his hand warm and firm on her elbow.

'Wrong way, *gattina.*'

Meghan jerked. 'What did you just call me?'

His lips quirked in a smile. '*Gattina.* It means kitten.'

'I don't like nicknames.'

'It was meant to be an endearment.'

'As in sex kitten?' she said contemptuously, and Alessandro shook his head.

'I was thinking more of an actual kitten, baring her tiny, tender claws.' He trailed his fingers from her elbow to her hand, stroking the tender palm, electrifying her skin with the lightest of touches. He raised her palm to his lips, gave it the barest brush of a kiss. A promise. Mesmerised, Meghan could only watch. And feel.

This was a bad, bad idea.

'This way,' Alessandro said, sounding faintly amused, and gestured to the other set of double doors leading into the foyer.

Numbly she followed Alessandro through the foyer and into a mahogany panelled dining room. Candles were lit, casting flickering shadows on the dark walls and tiled floor.

The green salad she'd seen earlier in the kitchen was now placed on an imposing table, one corner set intimately for two.

Meghan swallowed, and the gulping noise was loud in the room, where the only sound was the guttering of flame.

Alessandro laughed softly. 'Come here. I don't bite.'

Reluctantly Meghan moved towards him on wooden legs. 'Are you trying to seduce me?' she whispered. *Because it just might be working.*

'No. When I seduce you, you'll know.'

The languorous promise in these words sent both panic and anticipation fizzing through her in dangerous bubbles. 'I don't want to be seduced,' Meghan said, and knew how feeble her voice sounded.

'You don't want to be hurt,' Alessandro corrected. 'There's a difference.'

She lifted her chin. 'Is there?'

'I believe with me there is.' His voice, though gentle, allowed no argument. 'Now enough about seduction. Let us turn our attention to eating, which in Italy is just as sensual an art.'

Meghan sat at the table, watched as Alessandro poured wine from the bottle chilling in a bucket and served her a generous portion of salad bursting with tomatoes, basil and mozzarella.

'This looks delicious—thank you,' she murmured, and Alessandro smiled, a wicked, teasing glint in his eye.

'Is there anything else I may get for you? Ana will bring the antipasti later.'

With a start, Meghan realised Alessandro was the one serving her. Everything was mixed up tonight. She moved as if to get up, although she wasn't sure what she intended to do. Pour the water? Run to the kitchen? Curtsey?

He shook his head. 'The only thing I want you to do now, Meghan, is to enjoy.'

She opened her mouth to issue a sharp retort, the stinging reply that had become her habit, her defence. Alessandro watched her with an expectant little half-smile on his face, and Meghan hesitated.

She'd spent the last six months holding herself apart—apart from men, from pleasure, from life. Sometimes it felt as if it was the only way to get through each day—and, more importantly, to get back the dignity and self-respect she'd lost in Stanton Springs, Iowa.

Yet now, for one evening, even just one moment, she wanted to let go. Not completely, not out of control, because she knew she wasn't ready for that.

She just wanted to enjoy…something.

Food.

She sat back in her chair, managing a rather stiff-lipped smile. 'All right.' She took a bite of salad, felt the burst of tomato on her tongue. It felt different. Sweeter. The room seemed different. More vivid. And she felt different. More alive.

Alessandro watched her with an indulgent, affectionate smile, and Meghan took a sip of wine, the taste sharp and tangy.

Her senses were heightened to the feel of the cool, smooth wine glass in her fingers, the cotton shirt against her arms, her breasts. She saw Alessandro's languorous gaze, the way he watched her move, sleepily, yet with a flared awareness in his eyes that thrilled her.

This was so dangerous.

She knew Alessandro would not abuse her. He wouldn't spread malicious lies or treat her with cruel contempt.

But he would hurt her. Meghan put her wine glass down with an unsteady clatter. Yes, he would hurt her if she let him…if she gave him her heart.

Alessandro watched Meghan eat with a pleasure he normally reserved for more physical activities. He enjoyed seeing the way her eyes widened, the slow smile that spread over her features at the simplest of pleasures.

He'd no doubt that she was unaware of how sensual, how desirable she looked simply eating a tomato. She was, he was beginning to realise, quite unaware of her effect on him.

If only he was as unaware. The desire—the need—for her pulsed through him, an ache, a hunger that made him want. Yearn. He didn't like it. He didn't *want* to want anything—certainly not a woman from nowhere who looked at him with her heart in her eyes, shadowed by both fear and desire.

She was the last thing he needed.

Yet he wanted her.

And she wanted him. She was denying it with nearly every fibre of her being, but he saw the way she looked at him, the way her eyes flared and her lips parted.

She was afraid. The realisation humbled him. He would have to tread carefully.

Still, it was only a matter of time.

The thought pleased him, yet as he cradled his wine glass between his palms he felt a ripple of unease. Guilt.

He wasn't in the habit of buying women. And certainly not of lying to them. Since taking over Di Agnio Enterprises two years ago Alessandro had become known for his no-nonsense demeanour, as well as the brutal honesty he favoured with clients and friends alike.

Two years ago, on a chilly spring evening much like this one, he'd put away the trappings of a different life, the sweet-talking lies that had smoothed the already slippery path to pleasure.

He'd put them away for ever, even if some still wondered. Doubted.

Even if he did.

He lived for his work now, for seeing Di Agnio Enterprises rise in stature and earnings, for seeing his family name respected once more.

He did not live for pleasure.

He no longer cared about desire.

So why had he lured—and he knew that truly was the word for it—Meghan to his villa?

For seduction?

The thought made him frown, and he saw Meghan's gaze flicker uneasily over his countenance. She was as attuned to the variations of his mood as he was to hers.

He smiled. 'Have some pasta.' Ana had brought in the pasta dish a few moments earlier, her lips pressed in a thin line of disapproval, although she'd restrained herself from saying anything.

Alessandro had watched Meghan flush and look down at her plate, clearly embarrassed.

It was his fault she felt humiliated. He'd never meant her to feel so shamed, yet he knew he'd assumed things of her…things that he still wasn't sure were true or not.

Had he brought her here simply for pleasure?

For sex?

Was that what he wanted? Was that the kind of man he was…still?

He didn't know. Didn't know what to think of her, of himself. He took a sip of wine. When he'd seen her at Angelo's she'd seemed like any other of the many women he knew. Women who were free and easy with their favours, their bodies. There was no shame in that these days, although Alessandro recognised in himself a deep-seated disapproval of the freedom in women which he himself had enjoyed.

You didn't marry women like that.

He wouldn't marry a woman like that.

But was Meghan that kind of woman? He'd assumed it, and strangely *she* seemed to have assumed it.

But was it true?

And why had he brought her here?

Frowning again, Alessandro realised he couldn't answer those questions. Not yet. Which meant Meghan had to stay a bit longer. Until he discovered why he'd brought her here.

Until he discovered why he needed her.

CHAPTER FOUR

MEGHAN felt as if she were in a daze. Dazed by food, by wine, by pleasure. Drugged by her own senses and the novelty of letting herself feel…everything.

After their initial charged confrontation, Meghan found herself relaxing and enjoying the simple pleasure of conversation. She told Alessandro how she'd learnt Italian, and about some of her travels; he shared his experiences in the same places.

Meghan had to smile at the differences. She'd been slumming it with hostels and third-class train fares, while Alessandro travelled around Europe in a company jet, staying in five-star accommodation with a fresh magnum of champagne in every room.

And yet…they'd both found Notre Dame ostentatious, and fallen in love with the history of Père Lachaise, the famous Parisian cemetery. They'd both bypassed Brussels for Bruges, loving the historic city, with its church spires and cobbled streets.

Some things, Meghan thought, rose above money and status.

She found herself sneaking looks at him while he ate, watching the long, clean column of his throat as he sipped his wine, noticing the way his faded jeans moulded to his body as he sat, relaxed and half sprawled, in his chair. Watching his moods chase the colours in his eyes from navy to steel to indigo, a rainbow of blues.

Every movement, every look, every softly spoken word or dry chuckle, created a yearning in her soul—almost made her lean towards him, craving contact. Touch.

She wanted him.

Despite what he'd thought, despite what he still expected.
Despite the danger.

The realisation of her own need stunned her. She'd never
expected to feel the flooding, weakening sensation of desire
again. Never expected to want a man, to want to take pleasure
as well as to give it.

Her mind spun as she considered this, the novelty of reawak-
ening sensation, need. It was intoxicating. It was scary.

It was desire.

The shame that followed on its heels like a mocking shadow,
the fear she tasted in her mouth, were more familiar.

Meghan took a sip of wine, but it could have been water. A
pulse beat in her throat, and despite the liquid her mouth was dry.
She put the glass down carefully. 'I think I've had enough.'

Alessandro raised his eyebrows, waiting, sensing the
double entendre.

'It's late,' she continued stiltedly. 'I should go.'

'Go where?'

'You could drive me back to Spoleto.' Even as she said it,
Meghan knew it wasn't going to happen. Didn't want it to happen.

Alessandro smiled. 'I could.'

They were both silent. Meghan stared at her plate, at the
remains of one of the most delicious meals she'd ever had.
Silence thrummed between them—heavy, oppressive, expectant.

She looked up, her eyes wide, luminous. 'What happens
now?' she asked, her voice little more than a whisper.

Alessandro regarded her steadily. 'What do you want to
happen now?'

'I…' She licked her dry lips, resisting the urge to gulp down
the rest of her wine. 'I…I don't know.' The enormity of this admission caused a humiliating flush to steal across her cheeks. She
was as good as saying she wanted him.

And she *did* want him. Perhaps she even wanted him to know.
She stared at him now, openly, hungrily, wondering how hard and
broad his chest would feel against her own womanly softness,
how his mouth would feel on hers, covering it, possessing it, how
his hands would stroke and touch her body.

Wondering how sensual, how tender he would be.

Wondering how she would respond.

She wanted to know, and she was terrified.

Alessandro reached across the table to cover her hand with his own. 'Meghan, you may sleep in the spare bedroom. There need be nothing between us tonight.'

She was far too conscious of the heavy warmth of his hand on hers, the way it made tiny shocks ripple all the way up her arm. The strength of it, the security, the desire.

Tonight, she thought. The meaning was obvious. There would be another night, and perhaps another, and, if she were lucky, a few more.

And what then?

Could she really sell herself so cheaply simply for desire's sake?

Shame scorched her face, her soul.

'Tomorrow I leave,' she reminded him, although her words sounded hollow. 'Unless you plan to keep me here until… until…' She trailed off, courage deserting her.

Humour glinted in Alessandro's eyes. 'Maybe I do.'

'What if I say no?' Meghan demanded shakily. 'Are you going to force me?'

Alessandro swore softly. 'Do you think that is the kind of man I am? To force a woman? What has happened to you to think such things?' His eyes narrowed, though his voice was soft. 'Who was the man who hurt you, Meghan?'

The question echoed numbly through her, through the empty, scarred places inside. *The man who hurt you.* She stared down at her plate, the colours blurring into a sorrowful rainbow, her thoughts hopelessly scattered.

'You don't have to tell me if you don't want to,' Alessandro said quietly. 'But I think that it would help me to understand.'

Meghan forced herself to look up, blinking through a haze of devastated emotion and memory. 'What is there to understand?'

'Why you're so suspicious. Afraid. Ashamed.'

'I'm not!'

Alessandro simply inclined his head.

'Let's just say I'm coming out of a bad relationship,' she

finally managed. Meghan bit her lip, took in a shuddering breath. She felt cold, empty, even though the waves of emotion Alessandro had caused to crash through her still lapped at her nerves, her senses. 'Look, I'm suspicious, and I don't know what kind of man you are. You tricked me into coming here, after all.'

Alessandro's face was harsh in its sincerity. 'I promise you, I won't hurt you.'

'You might not mean to,' Meghan muttered.

His face blanked for a second, and he inclined his head in silent, brutal acknowledgement. Meghan looked down.

Alessandro leaned forward, rested a hand on her arm. His fingers were gentle, caressing, yet they burned. Made her ache, made her want to know how they would feel on her skin. All over her skin.

Meghan stared at his hand, the clean strength of it on her own pale fingers, as he murmured, 'Stay, Meghan. Spend the night—alone—and we can have the day tomorrow. To enjoy. Be tourists, if you like.'

'And see what happens?'

'Why must you think of the future? Let us just enjoy each other's company. It brings me pleasure to be with you, to look at you. Do you not feel the same?'

His voice was a caress, and Meghan found herself nodding, helpless. 'Yes…'

'Then let us enjoy it,' Alessandro said simply. 'Enjoy each other. And leave it at that.' He removed his hand, and Meghan felt bereft. Stupid to want his touch. Foolish to crave it when she knew it could only lead to hurt. Pain and shame.

'And then I leave,' she stipulated.

Alessandro shrugged. 'If that is your desire.'

'It is.'

'Very well.' He gazed at her, one hand curled around the stem of his wine glass, his eyes glittering.

'I'll sleep in the spare bedroom,' she said after a moment. He smiled and nodded.

'You know where it is? I can show you, if you like.'

'N-no,' she stammered. 'That's not necessary.'

He chuckled, enjoying her discomfiture. 'As you wish.'

Meghan lifted her chin. 'And I'll lock the door,' she added with her last mustered spirit, and for a moment Alessandro looked almost hurt.

'I'll take your word for it,' he said quietly.

The lights had been dimmed in her bedroom, the covers turned back. Meghan saw that a hot water bottle had been thoughtfully placed between the smooth cotton sheets and a nightgown—also cotton, and surprisingly modest—had been laid out on a chair.

She felt like a treasured guest. A captive guest. Yet she had chosen these bonds. She couldn't blame Alessandro any more.

This was her choice.

This was her desire.

Her hand hovered over the lock. She knew Alessandro would not try to come in; even to suggest it had been an insult. *She* was in control now.

Yet the fear she'd lived with for six long months was too deeply ingrained into her soul, her spirit. Biting her lip, Meghan turned the key, heard the audible click, and somehow knew Alessandro had heard it as well.

Too tired to think any more, to wonder what Alessandro intended to do or how she might respond, she changed and slipped into bed. Sleep blessedly came within a few minutes.

When she woke, sunlight was filtering through the linen curtains and casting shifting patterns on the floor.

Her eyes reminded him of sunlight.

Gilded words, or the truth? Meghan sighed and leaned back against the pillows. Her experience with Stephen had caused her to question everything that came out of a man's mouth, to think the worst of every admiring look he might give.

To doubt and to fear.

When would it stop? Meghan wondered. When would *she* stop? Yesterday morning she couldn't have imagined ever wanting a man again. She certainly couldn't have imagined the desire she would feel, as potent as a drug, as heady as new wine.

Desire.

Meghan closed her eyes. That was all it was. Desire. Sex. Not love.

Never love.

She could not, absolutely could not, fall in love with Alessandro di Agnio.

Love was dangerous. Love made you a fool and a victim.

Meghan was never going to fall in love again.

So, she thought with a rueful smile, all she needed to do was enjoy this day and make sure not to fall in love with Alessandro. Tonight she would leave Spoleto, and his life, for ever.

The thought made her wince. She wasn't ready to leave. How ridiculous, when only twelve hours ago she'd shrilly demanded her release.

Impatient with the thoughts chasing circles in her head, she threw off the covers. She would enjoy the day. Then she would say goodbye.

That was simply how it had to be.

A light knock sounded at the door, and Meghan whirled in surprise. 'Who is it?' she asked carefully, in Italian.

'Ana, *signorina*. I've brought you some clothes.'

'Just a moment...' Meghan hurried to the door and turned the key. 'Come in.'

The housekeeper bustled in, her expression ominously neutral as she placed a bundle of clothes on top of the bureau. 'Signor di Agnio thought you might wish for a change of clothes.'

'That was thoughtful of him.'

Ana inclined her head in what could have been a nod or a shrug. Her expression remained bland as she waited for Meghan's dismissal.

'Where did they come from?' Meghan asked, her curiosity piqued.

'The clothes?' Ana's mouth thinned in disapproval. 'They belong to Signor di Agnio's wife.'

'*What*?' Meghan stared at the housekeeper, her eyes wide with shock. Alessandro was *married*? 'His wife?' she repeated.

Ana inclined her head. 'Paula di Agnio. She lives in Rome.'

Married. Somehow Alessandro had forgotten to mention that little detail. Did he think it wasn't important? That she wouldn't care?

Meghan closed her eyes. *Liar*. She'd begun to believe Alessandro was different, that even if he only wanted sex at least he was honest about it.

He was a liar, like all the rest.

Like Stephen.

And she'd fallen for it, begun to believe his tender little act, because her heart and body still cried out for understanding, compassion.

Love.

No. Not that. Not that any more. Ever.

'Is there anything else you need, *signorina*?' Ana asked diffidently. 'There are toiletries in the bathroom. A toothbrush, deodorant—whatever you require.'

Meghan opened her eyes, blinking the room back into focus from behind the thick haze of tears that had come unbidden. 'Thank you.' Her voice came out rusty, and she cleared her throat. 'I'll be down shortly. Thank you for everything.'

Ana nodded, her expression still diffident, and left the room.

Meghan stared at the bundle of clothes. His wife's clothes. Did he actually think she would wear them? Could he judge her any lower?

Her mind still reeling from the housekeeper's unexpected news, Meghan dressed in her outfit from the previous night with numb, blunt fingers.

In the luxuriously appointed bathroom she found all the necessary toiletries, and was glad to wash her face and brush her teeth. As she stepped into the hallway she felt protected again, hardened enough to do battle.

To find out just what Alessandro had been keeping from her.

Her resolve wavered slightly when she stepped into the lounge and saw him waiting there. He turned when he saw her, and the spontaneous smile of affection and admiration made Meghan's heart stumble. Then his expression darkened.

'Why are you wearing your clothes from last night? Your…uniform?'

'Ana told me where the other clothes came from,' Meghan replied, her voice choked.

'Oh?' Alessandro's expression became guarded, a shutter closing over his eyes, turning them almost black, and Meghan's heart sank.

'Why didn't you tell me you were married?'

'*What*?' He stared at her incredulously, before suddenly laughing aloud, the sound pure and clean, filling the room. 'She told you that?'

'She said the clothes belonged to Signor di Agnio's wife.'

'Ah.' He nodded slowly, the laughter gone, not even an echo. 'Well, they do—but to a different Signor di Agnio's wife.'

Meghan stared at him in confusion. 'Who? Your father's?'

'My father is dead.' He bit out the words. 'The Signor di Agnio Ana was referring to is my brother. He was married to my sister-in-law, Paula.'

'Was?' she repeated uncertainly. 'Are they divorced?'

'No, my brother is also dead.' He paused, his eyes like iron as Meghan stared at him, unsure how to respond. 'This was his villa,' Alessandro continued. 'I use it for business purposes now.'

'Oh.' Meghan felt a blush crawl up her throat. 'I thought…'

'I know what you thought, *gattina*.' Amusement glittered in his cool eyes. 'You can sheath your little claws, because now you know Ana was just making trouble.'

'Why would she—?'

He cut her off swiftly, with a chuckle and a shake of his head. '*Da tutti i san*—you insist on thinking the worst of me at every turn! Married! What next?'

'I couldn't help it,' Meghan mumbled. 'Maybe I misunderstood the Italian…'

'Oh, really?' The look he gave her was far too perceptive. 'Tell me, this relationship you were in? Was the man married?'

Meghan's mouth was dry, her lips numb. 'I don't want to talk about it,' she finally managed.

He shrugged. 'Whoever he was, he has a lot to answer for. Now, I'm starving, and there is a full day before us. One without arguments, I hope. Why don't you get changed into the clothes that do not belong to my wife—a woman who does not yet exist—and meet me in the kitchen?'

The humour lighting his eyes made Meghan smile ruefully. Somehow Alessandro had dispelled the tension that had thrummed between them. She felt light, almost happy.

'All right,' she agreed, and hurried upstairs.

Back in the bedroom, Meghan tugged on a pair of designer jeans, a bit loose in the waist, but otherwise fitting her well, and a black cashmere turtleneck sweater. A leather belt fitted snugly around her hips, and she pulled her hair back with a clip.

She glanced in the mirror and was surprised to see her cheeks flushed, her eyes sparkling.

She looked like a woman on the brink of adventure. A woman desired.

Instead of the usual plunging fear in her belly at this thought, Meghan felt a warm tingling. A glow.

Smiling to herself, she headed down to the kitchen.

Thankfully Ana had disappeared, leaving them alone at the round pine table set in a comfortable nook overlooking the pool, still covered, and the terrace set with loungers and pots of flowers.

'It must be beautiful here in the summer,' Meghan said a bit wistfully, and Alessandro slotted her a thoughtful glance.

'It is. Now, eat.'

The food set before them was a feast. Meghan hadn't been overly fond of the Italian breakfasts she'd encountered so far, but set before her now was an array of mouthwatering dishes.

One eyebrow raised, Alessandro handed her a steaming bowl of eggs scrambled with mozzarella and basil. 'I prefer the full English breakfasts I had at school—done the Italian way, of course.'

'Of course.' Meghan helped herself to eggs, fresh orange juice, and toast with apricot preserve. 'Ana is a good cook,' she said, after the first few delicious mouthfuls.

'Who said Ana made it?' Alessandro challenged, and Meghan stared in surprise.

'You didn't...?'

'No, unfortunately you're right. I can't cook—more's the pity.' The smile tugging at Alessandro's mouth turned into a fully-fledged grin that made Meghan's answering smile die on her lips. Her throat was dry, her heart hammering.

She could not resist this man. Not when he smiled like that, his eyes warm, full of laughter, yet with heat just below the surface, simmering. Ready to blaze.

Meghan swallowed a mouthful of eggs and took a sip of orange juice, grateful to avoid Alessandro's gaze. He continued eating, and the rest of their breakfast passed with blessed uneventfulness.

'So,' Alessandro said a short while later, as he poured her a second cup of coffee, 'today I want to show you Umbria.'

'Which part?' Meghan asked, picking up the thick ceramic mug. The coffee was strong and smelled like heaven. She took a sip. 'I've seen Spoleto, of course, and Assisi.'

'We can take a driving tour. There are many beautiful sights in Umbria. Villages, mountains. Spoleto is lovely, but there are other hidden treasures. Treasures I want to show you.'

Meghan's hands tightened around her cup. She couldn't resist imagining a day out with him, basking in the spring sunshine, revelling in the mountain breeze. Holding hands, laughing over silly jokes. A proper date. Something normal people did. People who liked each other, who fell in love.

'It sounds lovely.' She hesitated, the escape clause she'd provided herself with still looming, a hopeless distraction. 'I still need to get my things.' Just thinking of Paulo, the hostel, even her haversack, seemed unreal. A different lifetime.

'I've sent for your things,' Alessandro replied with a dismissive shrug. 'They'll be in your room by this afternoon.'

Meghan put down her coffee cup with a clatter. 'You had no right—'

'Why must it be about rights? I did what was most convenient.'

'Convenient for *you*!'

Alessandro's eyes glittered. 'Are you going to fight me on every point? Or shall we enjoy the day together?'

Meghan sagged. He was right. She couldn't seem to get out of the battle stance—ready to doubt, to question, to attack. 'I'm sorry. That was…thoughtful of you.'

'Wasn't it?' He beamed at her. 'You're learning.'

Meghan gritted her teeth. 'Don't push it.'

Alessandro chuckled. 'I won't. I know well enough I need to take my time with you.'

It was a beautiful morning—perfect for driving through sun-touched hills—the sky a deep, pure blue, studded with fleecy clouds. The wind was chilly but the sun was warm, and Alessandro rolled down the windows so the breeze ruffled their hair as he drove down the steep, winding road away from Villa Tre Querce.

'I thought you'd be the kind of man to have a convertible,' Meghan admitted as they drove.

He glanced at her, his expression unreadable. 'I'm not quite sure what that says about your opinion of me. But I did have a convertible once.'

'What happened?' Meghan teased. 'You crashed it?'

'As a matter of fact, I did,' he replied flatly, staring straight ahead. Meghan opened her mouth to mumble some kind of apology, but the set of Alessandro's jaw made her close it again.

The day was too beautiful to dwell on anything unpleasant, and Meghan revelled in the sensual pleasure of wind and sun.

They drove for nearly an hour on twisting, narrow roads, up hills and through valleys, villages huddled on the distant mountains, the spire of a church's tower silhouetted against an azure sky.

At the base of a particularly steep hill Alessandro pulled the car over and killed the engine.

'Now we walk.'

'Walk?' Meghan held one hand over her eyes to shade them from the sun as she squinted up at road ahead of them, twisting steeply upwards into nowhere. 'What's up there?'

'You'll see.'

She took his hand, warm, dry, strong, liking the way his hand encased hers.

'Close your eyes.'

'What?' She jerked in surprise, withdrawing her hand by instinct, but Alessandro held onto it. His thumb caressed her palm, and Meghan suppressed a shiver, affected by the simple touch. 'Why should I close my eyes?' she asked.

'Just do it.' Alessandro paused, his eyes dark, intent. 'Please. Trust me.'

Trust him? Every instinct in her rebelled. She didn't *do* trust. Except something deep within her heart, her soul, wanted her to trust this man.

And that was the most frightening thing of all.

Meghan glanced up at the road, at Alessandro's steady gaze, then finally shrugged and laughed.

'Why not?' she said lightly, and, closing her eyes, let him lead her as if she were a child.

The road was steep, and with her eyes closed Meghan felt as if she could tumble backwards into an abyss at any moment. Alessandro tugged gently on her hand, leading her onwards, upwards.

'Keep them closed,' he ordered sternly, and a bubble of laughter escaped her.

'I'm trying.' She stopped for a moment, chest heaving. 'I'm also out of breath. I'm not used to this kind of hiking.'

'I thought you'd been travelling around Europe.'

'My general mode of transportation has been train or bus,' Meghan returned tartly, 'and I stick to the cities. I haven't been wandering out in the hills like some Umbrian nomad!'

He chuckled softly. 'Now's your chance.'

With her eyes closed she was all the more conscious of the sun warm on her face, the dry scent of pine and cypress mixed with the heady fragrance of wild lavender and rosemary.

She was also exquisitely, achingly conscious of Alessandro's hand encasing hers, the way his fingers held hers lightly yet with such certainty, such possession. The way the simple touch seemed to reach inside and touch her where she was most vulnerable, most needy.

Her heart. Her mind. Her soul.

'Are we almost there yet?' she asked, her voice coming out in a rusty croak. She tried instinctively to pull her hand away, but Alessandro's grip only tightened.

'Don't be frightened.'

'Who said I was scared?'

'I can tell. We're almost there.'

Wherever 'there' was. Since they'd been walking she hadn't

heard another person or even a car in the distance. The only sound was the wind in the trees and the faint tinkling of a far-off goat's bell.

'Can you hear it?' Alessandro asked softly.

Meghan strained to listen, and realised she could now hear in the distance what sounded like rushing wind. The light breeze caressing her face could hardly cause such a sound, and she shook her head in confusion. 'Yes, but what is it?' She started to open her eyes again, only to have Alessandro cover them with his hand.

'Don't spoil it,' he murmured. 'A little bit longer.'

The feel of his hand on her face, his thumb reaching down to caress her cheek, her lips, made Meghan stumble. Gently Alessandro tugged on her hand until she came forward, and he wrapped his arm around her waist, pulling her against him, her back against his chest, his other hand still covering her eyes.

'Let me go,' Meghan said breathlessly, even as desire—forbidden, treacherous, molten—coursed through her veins.

'I don't want to.'

'What about what I want?'

'But I don't think you want me to, either.' She could sense rather than see his smile. His hand still covered her eyes, his fingers brushing over her cheeks, her chin, her lips, as if he were memorising the touch of her. The feel of her.

She sagged against him. She couldn't help it. His chest was hard, unyielding, and yet she still seemed to mould herself to his contours. She felt the betraying hardness of his own desire against her back, and it only made her want to press closer.

Her insides were turning to liquid; a pulse deep inside was thrumming to life. Her breath hitched and his thumb traced her half-open lips, ran along her teeth.

His own breath feathered her hair, and he tilted her head upwards, still covering her eyes, and brushed her lips in the soft kiss of an angel.

Meghan's lips parted soundlessly, helplessly, and he deepened the kiss, turned it into something achingly sweet, wonderfully gentle.

Desire was flickering, licking through her, weakening both

her limbs and her resolve. She reached up with her fingers, tugged at the hand that covered her eyes.

She wanted to look at him, and yet the feel of his lips plundering hers was so exquisite she didn't want it to stop.

'Alessandro…' It came out as a whisper, a plea.

He chuckled.

She jerked back slightly, still caught in his embrace, his hand still covering her eyes. 'You think this is funny?'

'A bit,' Alessandro replied, unperturbed. 'But enough. I want you to see me when I make love to you. I want you to look into my eyes and see how I want you.'

He paused, his thumb outlining the fullness of her mouth again. Meghan's lips parted in silent invitation. She couldn't help it.

'And I want to see in your eyes how you want me.'

He removed his hand from her waist and led her onwards once more. 'Keep them closed,' he warned, and dropped his hand from her face.

Meghan longed to open her eyes—if just to see the expression on Alessandro's face. Smug because he'd made her want him so easily? Would there be the residual flicker of desire in own brilliant eyes?

Somehow she kept them closed. It had become a matter of pride. Of trust.

He tugged her along the stony path and she followed, her limbs still weak, flooded with sensation. With need.

Alessandro had recovered from their kiss more quickly than she had, she thought ruefully.

He held her hand gently, helping her over rocks and twisted roots. Meghan clung to him, moving carefully over the unfamiliar ground.

The rushing sound had become increasingly louder with every step, and when Alessandro finally brought her to a stop it was a roaring in her ears. She could feel the spray of water on her face.

'Now open them.'

Meghan obeyed, and found herself staring at a magnificent waterfall, a pure cascade of rushing whiteness that dropped over a hundred metres into a restless surging river below.

She clapped her hands in delighted surprise. 'A waterfall! I'd no idea!'

'Cascata delle Marmore. It's beautiful, isn't it?' Alessandro leaned against the balustrade of the viewing balcony he'd brought her to. The waterfall was like a huge sheet of streaming glass, surrounded by dense green foliage and trees. Meghan felt as if she were on a tropical island, despite the cool breeze teasing her hair into her eyes.

She stared at the water, rushing blue-green turning to pure white foam. It was both beautiful and frightening in its sheer power. 'I didn't realise there were natural waterfalls in this part of Italy,' she marvelled.

'It's not actually natural,' Alessandro told her. 'The Romans built it nearly two thousand years ago. They created viaducts to drain off the swampy land around the River Velino and pour the excess water off the Marmore Cliff into the Nera. Now it's only turned on for a few hours a day. The rest of the time it's little more than a trickle.'

'You mean it's not real?' She felt a twinge of disappointment that this powerful beauty hadn't been here since time began. Wasn't even *meant* to be here.

Alessandro turned to her, one eyebrow raised. 'What's real?' He gestured to the falls, raising his voice over the sound of rushing water to be heard. 'That looks rather real to me.'

'I suppose you're right,' Meghan said slowly. 'I certainly wouldn't want to go over it in a barrel!' she joked, then shook her head. 'I don't know—somehow it would be more impressive if it hadn't been manufactured by man.'

'Isn't that what makes it so amazing?' Alessandro countered. 'It was a swamp, a stagnant river—useless, dangerous, even— and they made it into something beautiful.'

'And still dangerous,' Meghan couldn't resist saying.

'Yes. Still dangerous.'

What were they really talking about? The falls, or something deeper? An even stronger current that threatened to pull her under, drowning her self-respect, her independence, and leaving only need.

A current that, like the falls, had been manufactured, created by an impossible and unreal situation.

Currents like that couldn't last. What was once a torrent would become a trickle, turned off at the source, by the source.

Alessandro. This was his game, she knew, and he was calling all the shots. He was in control.

Just one day, she reminded herself. One day couldn't be dangerous.

Except perhaps it could, with Alessandro.

'Come on.' Alessandro put an arm around her shoulders easily, as naturally as if he'd done it many times before. 'We can have lunch in Montefranco.'

Back in the car, he gave her a knowing glance. 'Still disappointed the falls aren't real?'

She shrugged. 'I can't deny they were beautiful.'

'Do you know the story behind them? Nera was a wood nymph who fell in love with a shepherd boy. The goddess Juno was jealous, so she turned Nera into a river.'

'The River Nera,' Meghan surmised. 'Bad luck for her, falling in love with the wrong man.'

'Perhaps,' Alessandro conceded with a wry smile. 'But do you know what her shepherd Velino did?'

'Found a shepherdess?'

He chuckled softly. 'No, he was so anguished at the loss of his love, he threw himself off the Marmore Cliff. His tears became the waterfall, and so they are joined for ever, the Rivers Velino and Nera. Their love lasting into eternity.'

Meghan smiled tightly. 'A sweet story.'

'You don't believe in lasting love?' There was a cynical edge to his voice that was impossible to miss.

'No, I don't,' Meghan said baldly. 'Do you?'

Something flickered in his eyes—disappointment? Relief? Who knew? Meghan looked out of the window, refusing to be drawn in. It didn't matter what Alessandro thought about everlasting love, because there was nothing *lasting* about their situation.

'No,' he said after a moment. 'No, Meghan. In that respect I'm like you.'

And, strangely, Meghan suddenly felt sad for them both.

Two people together, bound by desire and disillusion.

Montefranco was one of Umbria's classic hillside towns, its houses and churches perched on the green slopes as if they'd sprung up from the soil. Alessandro led her to a little trattoria tucked away on a narrow cobbled street, and the proprietor, a jolly man in an apron-covered suit, greeted him like a friend. After speaking briefly in his usual rapid-fire Italian, Alessandro slowed down to introduce Meghan.

'Antonio—my friend from America—Meghan Selby.'

He made her sound like a pen-pal. Smiling, Meghan shook the older man's hand. Yet how else could he possibly explain her presence?

It didn't make sense. This entire day didn't make sense. It was something out of a story, a fantasy, and it would end tonight.

Meghan's mouth turned dry. Tonight…when she walked away with a wave and a smile. If she could.

And if she couldn't…?

'You know what they say,' Antonio said, 'a friend of Alessandro di Agnio's is a friend of mine.' He turned to Alessandro, still speaking slowly for Meghan's benefit. 'So good to see you! It's been too long.'

'I've been busy, Antonio,' Alessandro said as he clapped the older man on the shoulder.

'I know! I know! All this work in the city—no time for rest, for play. I never thought I would say that to you, of course…' His chuckle faltered at Alessandro's wintry look.

'You along with many others.' He smiled, but it was as if a light had gone out in his eyes, turning them from blue to lifeless black.

'The poached cod is delicious,' Alessandro told her after they'd both silently perused the menus. 'If you care for fish.'

Meghan grimaced. 'Sorry, I'm a smalltown girl from the Midwest. I'm not much of a one for seafood.'

He chuckled. 'How about the *strascinati* with black truffle sauce? The truffles are famed in this region. It's a long-guarded secret where you can find them.'

'Do you know?' she asked, and Alessandro gave an eloquent, arrogant shrug that forced an unwilling laugh from her lips.

'Of course. You must try the *vino santigrano* as well. It's made locally, from some of the best vineyards in all of Italy.'

'Sounds like you know the menu,' Meghan commented. 'Do you come here often?'

'Do you mean, do I bring all my women here?' Alessandro said, his eyes alight with rueful humour.

'Something like that.' She smiled in admission, a tell-tale blush stealing across her cheeks.

'I told you—I like food.'

It was, she realised, not an answer to her question. How many women had he had? He was a man who knew women, who understood them, who was made for lovers...if not for love.

Alessandro steered the conversation into calmer waters, regaling her with tales and antics of the Umbrian locals, peppered with the mythology of the region.

Antonio himself brought the food and poured the wine, and Meghan could feel herself relaxing, enjoying. Laughing. Flirting.

'Try this.' Antonio had laid a sumptuous-looking rolled pastry on the table between them, and now Alessandro lifted a forkful to Meghan's lips.

Closing her eyes, she opened her mouth, and Alessandro slid a forkful of heaven inside.

The taste of chocolate, raisins and walnut melted onto Meghan's tongue. It was delicious. It felt like a sin. 'Mmm...what *is* this?'

'*Attorta*...a speciality of Umbria.'

Meghan opened her eyes to find Alessandro smiling at her, his gaze heavy-lidded, languorous. Sensual.

The pastry turned tasteless in her mouth, her throat so dry she could barely swallow.

Desire pulsated between them, coiled around Meghan's heart, her lungs, until she found she couldn't breathe. When she finally managed to drag air in, her breath came out in a shudder.

Alessandro smiled. 'Have another bite.'

Obediently, Meghan opened her mouth, and Alessandro slid

in another forkful. She could feel a drip of chocolate on the corner of her mouth and, mesmerised, watched as Alessandro wiped it before licking it off his own finger.

'Mmm.'

She closed her eyes briefly. 'What's going on here?' she whispered.

'We're eating dessert.'

'Alessandro, you know what I mean.'

He shrugged, though his eyes blazed into hers. 'I want you. You want me.'

'It's not that simple.'

'Isn't it?'

Meghan shook her head. 'I wish it were.' She gazed down at the crumbled remnants of their shared feast, delicious while it lasted but gone so quickly. She'd travelled that route before.

She would not do it again.

She looked up, her eyes wide and bleak. 'I won't sleep with you.'

'So you've said.' Alessandro took a sip of wine, looking amused.

Meghan sighed wearily. 'I know you think you'll wear me down eventually, and in truth you might get close. You might even win.'

'Is this a battle?' he murmured.

'You know it is. If I sleep with you I'll lose my self-respect, my dignity. I'll have given into desire, and I'll hate myself for it.'

'Why couch it in those terms? Why can't we love each other as two responsible, mature adults?'

Meghan laughed without humour. 'Because it's not about *love*.'

'You said you didn't believe in love.'

There was no mistaking the look of surprise on Alessandro's face, the heavy-lidded languor replaced with a wary tension.

'I don't. That doesn't mean I'm going to give myself to every—any—man I'm attracted to. I don't operate that way. Sorry.'

'So. You don't believe in love, but you won't make love with someone out of simple desire. What are you going to do? Become a nun?'

Meghan gave a shaky laugh. 'At times that prospect is appealing.' She twirled her fork between her fingers. 'I don't know what is going to happen in the future.' Her tone and face were bleak as she considered the prospect. The future was something she avoided thinking about. Sometimes it didn't seem as if she had one at all. 'I just can't ever see myself falling in love again. If that means being alone, then I guess I'll just have to get used to that.'

'It's not easy, being alone,' Alessandro said after a moment.

Meghan glanced at him, surprised by the guarded note in his voice, the vulnerability in his eyes. 'Sometimes it's safer.'

He nodded thoughtfully. 'Safety is important to you?'

'Yes.'

'This man you were with—you loved him? And he made you feel unsafe?'

'Of course he did,' Meghan replied shortly. 'Stephen was married. I didn't know it—'

'Stephen?' Alessandro's eyes darkened. He reached across the table to pluck the fork from her hand. He took her fingers in his, stroking her wrist with soft, tender movements. 'This Stephen— he was an ass. Even I can see that. But you can't let one man— one experience—spoil the rest of us for ever.'

'I'm sure,' Meghan said with a little smile, struggling to hold onto her composure as the fluttery little movements on her wrist went straight to her heart, 'you'd like to be the man to break the pattern.'

'One man, one relationship, is not a pattern.'

'Well, no.' Meghan glanced down, her eyes suddenly blurred with tears as memories rushed to the surface—memories she had firmly stamped down when she'd fled Stephen's apartment, fled the memories and the tears and kept running.

She still hadn't stopped.

'Meghan? *Gattina*?' Alessandro lifted her chin with his fingertips. 'What is wrong? What did I say?'

'Nothing.' Meghan blinked back the tears and smiled. 'I'm sorry.'

'No, I am sorry. We've wasted enough time indoors. We can walk through the town, up to the old fortress. There is a beautiful view from its walls.'

And as easily as that, he dispelled the tension, the sorrow.

Meghan let herself be led, her hand in his, out into the Umbrian sunshine.

The last thing she wanted to think about was Stephen, or the night she'd finally had the courage to walk away.

That was a memory she had locked deep into her soul. Something she never, never wanted to talk about. Certainly not to Alessandro. Not to anyone. Ever.

The fortress was built into the hill, overlooking the tumbled buildings of the town, and Meghan could imagine how it had once been formidable, impenetrable.

Now its walls were crumbling, mellow in the sunshine, and children played in the street below. Meghan let Alessandro lead her up the steps onto the top of the crenellated wall, the Umbrian countryside spread out before them in a peaceful patchwork of earthen colours.

A teasing wind blew her hair around her face and she breathed in the clean, pine-scented air, as pure and satisfying as a drink of water.

Alessandro and Meghan silently surveyed the panorama of tumbled hills and olives groves, taking in the majesty of an unchanged landscape.

'Did you grow up here?' Meghan asked after a long moment.

'Yes and no. As I told you, I went to school in England. My parents' main house of residence is in Milan. And yet...' He smiled with wry honesty. 'This was home.'

'Your brother's villa?'

'Yes. It was my father's before that.'

But not yours, Meghan realised silently, wondering what lay behind his careful choice of words.

'Well, it's beautiful,' she said with a smile. 'I happened on Spoleto by chance, but I'm glad I came.'

'So am I,' Alessandro murmured, and sudden expectant tension thrummed between them, heavy with meaning, with possibility.

Meghan stared out at the countryside, blind now to its charms.

'I should take you back to Spoleto tonight,' Alessandro said suddenly. His face looked hard.

Meghan's stomach plunged icily. She realised she was disappointed. She had expected to stay. She'd expected Alessandro to want her to stay.

'If that's what you want,' she said, only just managing to keep her voice steady.

Alessandro raked a hand through his hair. 'You know it is not!' He dropped his hand, tracing her cheek with his fingers. 'But you are haunted, Meghan, by the past. This man—he is like a shadow. I can almost see him at your shoulder.'

Meghan touched his fingers briefly with her own, her fingers winding around his, clinging. Pleading. 'I don't want him there.'

Alessandro smiled sadly. 'Neither do I.'

He cupped her cheek and she closed her eyes, revelling in the touch, the tenderness. She couldn't go yet. She couldn't leave this man—this hold he had on her senses, her soul. Perhaps even her heart. It wasn't love. She knew that. It was desire; it was need.

'Don't take me back yet,' she whispered.

His hand stilled. 'Are you sure?'

Meghan opened her eyes, swallowed audibly. Panic was fast setting in. 'I don't mean… I'm not…'

Alessandro smiled. His thumb caressed her lips. 'I know.'

He drew her naturally to him, in an embrace that was gentle rather than passionate. 'Stay,' he murmured against her hair. 'God knows, I don't want you to go.'

Meghan knew their time had been extended by only a day, perhaps two. Soon she would have to move on, and so would Alessandro. Their lives had never been meant to intertwine.

This was going to end. It was just a matter of when…and what happened beforehand.

The drive back to Tre Querce was quiet, both of them lost in their own thoughts. Meghan gazed out of the window at the fallow fields and bare vineyards, the sky above streaking lavender and gold.

She'd never reacted to any man the way she reacted to Alessandro—even Stephen hadn't affected her so profoundly, so deeply…as if he were stroking not just her hand or her body, but her soul.

Her whole body—her whole self—yearned towards his touch, his understanding. The two, she realised, were intimately connected.

He didn't love her.

He made no promises.

And yet…she wanted him.

She *wanted* him.

More than she'd ever wanted anything in her whole life.

More than your self-respect?

Meghan closed her eyes against the setting sun now blazing over the hills and fields.

I don't know.

As Alessandro turned the car up the twisting drive, Meghan wondered what the night would hold. She turned to look at him, and he sensed her gaze and smiled, reaching over to twine her fingers with his.

'Don't be afraid, Meghan. There don't have to be any shadows.'

Shadows. Meghan thought of Stephen. She could still see his face, hear his words.

I thought this was what you wanted.

How could he have thought that? How could he have twisted everything so horribly, so shamefully?

Alessandro was nothing like him, Meghan told herself. She knew that. He'd proved it to her again and again over this day. No matter how they'd started—what she'd thought—what *he'd* thought—it was different now.

Everything was different.

Could be different…if she let it.

If she let the shadows fade away.

Alessandro's hand tightened briefly on her own. 'Ana has the night off.'

So they would be alone. Meghan swallowed. 'Alessandro, I want—'

Meghan broke off, her heart still hammering, as Alessandro braked sharply in front of Tre Querce and cursed in Italian under his breath.

There was another car parked in front of the villa, a racy red convertible, and the man leaning against its hood was one Meghan recognised.

It was Alessandro's companion from lunch at Angelo's. As the man's eyes flashed to Meghan her own stomach lurched. There was no mistaking his knowing, lascivious grin or what it meant.

CHAPTER FIVE

'WELL, well, well.' Richard Harrison pushed himself away from the convertible and strolled towards Alessandro's car. 'You sly dog. Keeping her all to yourself.'

Alessandro flicked a cool, contemptuous gaze towards Richard. 'I don't recall inviting you here,' he replied, in a voice of dangerous silkiness.

'I was bored, and I do believe it's your job to entertain me.'

'You're not a child, Richard, as much as you behave like one.'

Richard's watery blue eyes blazed for a second. His mouth turned down sulkily. 'You need my business, di Agnio.'

Alessandro chuckled dryly, although his expression remained diamond-hard. 'You should realise by now, Richard, that there are very few things I need. You and your string of second-rate department stores is not one of them.'

Richard's face suffused with colour, turning puce. He clenched his fists, half raised one. 'You'll regret that.'

'I don't think so.'

Meghan's hand was slippery on the door handle as she grasped it. She heard the men trading insults, but it sounded like no more than dogs snarling at one another. She couldn't take it in. The one salient detail that had made its way into her numb mind was Richard's careless sentence.

Keeping her all to yourself.

They'd discussed her. Talked about her.

Richard's gaze roved over Meghan with crude, insulting

boldness, his eyes lingering on her breasts and thighs, sweeping over her as if he owned her, as if she could be bought. His thin lips turned up in a revolting smirk, and his watery eyes gleamed with lust. 'She's just as pretty as I said.'

'I think you should leave, Richard.' Alessandro's voice was calm and dispassionate, but a muscle ticked in his jaw and his eyes were like black ice.

Richard raised his eyebrows. 'What was it you said? There are better amusements in Spoleto than a two-bit part-time whore? It seems there aren't, my friend, and I think it's time you started to share.' He moved towards her, pale eyes glittering, and Meghan couldn't move. Couldn't think except to hear the sickening echo of his words.

Alessandro's words.

Two-bit part-time whore.

Just as she'd suspected and Alessandro had denied.

Just as she'd *known*.

She watched, transfixed, trapped, as Richard reached for her, his wet lips parted, his eyes glittering with lecherous intent.

He never managed to touch her. Alessandro moved with swift, calm certainty.

She heard rather than saw the crunch of Alessandro's fist into Richard's jaw. He staggered and fell onto the pavement by her feet.

She stared down silently. She still hadn't moved.

'I could sue you!' Richard choked. He clutched at his bleeding mouth, his face contorted with humiliated fury.

Alessandro massaged his knuckles. There was a fierce, primal light of satisfaction burning in his eyes as he gazed down at Richard. 'I don't think so,' he said calmly. 'Now, you'd better get off my premises before I do something worse to that pathetic baby face of yours.'

Richard glared. 'You've just lost a hell of a lot of business, di Agnio. I know what this deal meant to Di Agnio Enterprises!'

Alessandro's smile was sardonic. 'I'll live.' He turned his back on Richard in dismissal, and put his arm around Meghan's shoulders. 'Are you all right?'

'I'm fine.' Her voice came out as brittle and sharp as shattered glass. She *felt* as if she were nothing more than a handful of shattered glass, a fistful of jagged splinters. Shaking off Alessandro's arm, she moved towards the villa. 'I'll just get my things.'

She walked on numb legs to her room, the villa streaming by her blind eyes in a blur of colour.

Almost dispassionately she saw that her haversack had been placed at the foot of her bed. Who had fetched it? she wondered. How many minions worked for Alessandro, in a life she didn't even understand, with a power she could not begin to fathom? A power abused.

She stuffed her crumpled white shirt and black skirt into the bag. She could return the clothes she was wearing to Alessandro later. There was no time to change.

She was zipping up her bag when Alessandro strode into the room.

'What the hell are you doing?'

In the distance she heard the roar of the convertible heading down the drive. She spoke through stiff lips. 'Leaving.'

'Just like that?'

'Just like that.' Meghan tugged at the zipper of her bag, refusing to meet Alessandro's eyes. She couldn't do that and get out of here. She knew she couldn't.

'You can't.'

'Yes, I can.' *Barely.* The zipper had finally closed, and she swung the haversack onto her shoulder. She still hadn't looked at him.

It was the only way she could keep the desperate shards of self-respect and sanity together.

For surely if she stayed one moment longer than necessary—if she let Alessandro talk to her, touch her—they would be scattered.

Stolen.

'If you won't drive me, I'll walk.'

'It's over five kilometres to Spoleto,' Alessandro warned. His mouth was a thin line of anger, his eyes black, his body tense and ready to spring, although there was a loose-limbed grace to his movements even in his fury.

Meghan shook her head wearily. 'You can't keep me prisoner here, Alessandro.'

'Were you prisoner at the falls? At lunch? With me all day? When you begged me to let you stay? Don't throw that one at me this time, Meghan. It won't work.'

'I enjoyed today,' Meghan said, with a dispassionate calm she was far from feeling. 'But I didn't *beg*.' She felt sick, and she prayed she wouldn't throw up. Prayed she wouldn't cry. 'Now I want to leave.'

'No.'

'I'll walk—'

'No.' He took her gently by the shoulders, his touch like a promise. Meghan closed her eyes. She didn't need this. Couldn't need it.

When he spoke his voice was a caress. 'Look at me, Meghan.'

Damn him. Unwillingly, despite every good intention she'd ever had, she met his eyes.

'Why are you doing this? Is it because of Richard? He's a pig—*porca*—'

'Two-bit, part-time whore.' The words came out in a sorry little whisper.

Alessandro stared at her, his eyes blazing, filled with an urgency that almost undid her.

'You believe what he said?' he finally demanded hoarsely.

Meghan spoke through numb lips, her voice a rusty whisper. 'Tell me it isn't true. Tell me you didn't say it.'

Alessandro was silent, his gaze hard and unyielding. Then he released her, running a hand through his hair, and Meghan sagged against the bed. Her haversack fell to the floor.

'I did say it.'

Tears pricked her lids. She'd begun to think perhaps it wasn't true. Only now did she realise how much that brief flicker of hope had cost her. Damn him. Damn him for making her feel.

Feel so very much.

'But I didn't know you then,' Alessandro continued in a voice of determined calm.

Meghan tossed her head, blinking back tears. 'It was *yesterday*, Alessandro.'

'A day is a long time.'

'Not long enough.' And yet far too long.

One day wasn't supposed to be dangerous.

And yet it was. It *was*.

Wearily, every limb leaden, she stooped to pick up her haversack.

'What do you want from me?' Alessandro demanded. 'Complete trust—faith in you before I even know you?'

She shook her head. 'Don't you see? You judged me then, in the restaurant.'

'Fine. I admit it. So?' He stared at her, head tilted with casual instinctive arrogance, eyes blazing blue fire. 'Harrison liked the look of you. He wanted to invite you here to serve us and see what happened.'

Meghan swallowed painfully. 'And that's just what you did.'

'It is not! I rejected his offer—coldly, in disgust. Yes, I called you a two-bit part-time whore. I admit it, and I will not apologise. I didn't know you then—hadn't spoken to you, hadn't looked into your eyes.' His own eyes burned now into hers. 'And when I did I wanted you. I wanted you for myself. Not as a waitress. Not as a whore. As a woman.'

'Yet when you first invited me here you *did* think that of me…didn't you? It wasn't until later—'

'What does it matter when it was?' Alessandro exclaimed. 'We are arguing about details!'

'No,' Meghan said, her voice stronger now. 'We're not. All that lovely nonsense about a pretty girl and wanting to get to know her, needing a pretence because of your prestige and wealth—it was just that. Nonsense. Lies. You didn't mean any of it.'

'I did.'

'Don't lie to me!' Meghan's voice rose in frustrated anger. She wanted truth—at least now. She deserved that much. 'I thought you were honest. I was beginning to believe— But you're as low and slimy as every other man I've known, thinking I'm a slut without even knowing my name! Lying to me to get what you want!'

'Don't compare me to that filth who used you,' Alessandro warned in a dangerous voice. 'I've been very patient with you, Meghan.'

She laughed incredulously, and the sound turned into a sneer. 'Patient? Waiting twenty-four hours before you demand to be serviced? *I don't think so.*'

Alessandro's face was white with anger. 'Have I demanded *anything* from you?' he asked, in a low voice that still managed to thrum with power.

'Should I be thankful?' Meghan snarled back, too hurt to care how she sounded, how her words might hurt. She wanted them to hurt. She wanted, savagely, to bring Alessandro as low as he'd brought her, though she doubted it was possible. He didn't care what she thought. He didn't care what she felt. 'I won't be your night-time entertainment,' she declared.

'As I recall, you haven't been providing any such entertainment,' Alessandro retorted, his voice a predatory hiss. 'Perhaps that's the problem.' He moved towards her with slow, purposeful strides, and the sudden intent look in his eyes, the harsh lines of his face softening with deliberate languor, made Meghan step backwards and stumble against the bed.

'Don't touch me!'

Alessandro prowled closer, an elegant stalking beast. Meghan pressed further against the bedframe, her heart thudding so hard she could feel the blood rushing in her ears.

She fell backwards onto the mattress, throwing one hand out to keep herself from becoming entirely helpless before him.

'I'm not going to touch you,' Alessandro informed her silkily. He stood above her, hands on hips, his whole body radiating lithe power, raw hunger.

His eyes glittered with intent and Meghan lay there, helpless, trapped by her own damning need.

'I'm not that kind of man. But I am going to tell you how I *would* touch you if you let me. If you wanted me to.'

Meghan opened her mouth soundlessly, her eyes wide.

'Do you know how I would touch you, Meghan? No, of course you don't. I don't think you've ever been touched that way. I imagine the man who took your innocence—because he did, didn't he?—I imagine he used you for his own pleasure. He didn't think about your needs—your desires—at all. Am I right?'

She wanted to speak. She *would* speak. She would tell him to go to hell, and then she would get up and walk away.

Except she didn't.

'When I touch you, Meghan,' Alessandro continued, his voice a caressing whisper, 'you'll want me to. You'll want me to because you'll know that I want you, and you can want me, and that it can be *good*. Nothing shameful, nothing sordid.'

'No…' It came out as a plea, although whether to stop or continue Meghan didn't even know. She was mesmerised by his words, by the unabashed hunger in his eyes, the desire he was not afraid to show.

The desire he was not afraid to feel.

'First I'll touch your lips. I've touched them already…just a taste. I want more now. I want more of you.' He paused thoughtfully, his eyes glittering. 'I think I'll love touching your lips. They're soft, and they'll taste of walnut and raisins. Like the *attorta* we shared. Do you remember? Nutty and moist and so very, very sweet.' His eyes moved from her mouth to her throat, and Meghan felt the damning blush staining her skin. Giving him evidence.

'I'll touch your throat there, where I can see your pulse. It's beating quite wildly now.' He smiled, and Meghan saw the desire in his eyes—pure, blazing. Elemental. 'Then I'll move lower. I'll touch your breasts. I wonder what they look like? As golden as the rest of you? I want to feel them in my hands.' He raised his hands, palms upwards, cupped, and Meghan moved slightly, leaning towards him, craving the thought of his touch.

'I'll touch you everywhere,' Alessandro continued, his voice ragged now. 'Stroking and kissing and bringing you to heights you've never climbed, places you've never been. Shattering you into a thousand pieces and then putting you back together again. And then you'll touch me.'

Meghan shuddered. She couldn't help it.

'You'll touch me, and I'll want you to touch me. It will be like a gift.' He closed his eyes briefly, his expression straining, pained. 'I want that very much, Meghan. I want you to touch me.'

He stood very still, his head thrown back, the column of his throat brown and exposed and clean. Then he lowered his head and opened his eyes. Meghan saw the naked vulnerability there. He'd bared himself to her, she realized.

No other man had given her so much while seeming to promise so little.

He'd given her control. It felt precious.

Slowly, her legs trembling, she stood up. She was so close to him she could feel his breath on her cheek. Still he did not move.

Her hand shook as she lifted it, placed it deliberately on his chest. She could feel his heartbeat race under her palm, the muscles jerk in response, and a little smile stole over her features.

'You see what you do to me?' Alessandro's voice was choked.

Meghan looked up. There was so much in his eyes—so much need, so much pain, so much desire. It stunned her, left her breathless.

And yet he didn't move. His whole body was taut, straining, still.

She slid her hand up, across the solid width of his chest, along his neck, letting her fingers coil in the crisp curls of hair at his nape.

He remained motionless, though his breathing was uneven, ragged.

She stood on her tiptoes, using her hands to pull his face down to hers. She brushed her lips against his, surprised at their softness, daring him, willing him to respond.

He moved.

His arms came around her, drawing her to his hard length with a gentleness that still gave witness to his urgency. His mouth turned the barest brush of a kiss into something far deeper and more demanding.

Meghan surrendered.

She didn't know how they got to the bed, how they ended up lying in a tangle of limbs until she wasn't sure where she ended and Alessandro began. His hands were on her, hot, sure, seeking. She felt him smile against her throat as he reached to cup the fullness of one breast.

'You're so beautiful.'

Meghan let her own hands roam along the smooth expanse of

his back. When had he taken off his shirt? She didn't know if she'd taken it off; everything was a softened haze of desire, of need.

Nothing mattered but this moment, this time of touch and taste and feel.

Oh, how she felt.

She felt his hands as they slid across her stomach, temptingly lower. She felt his lips as they traced a fiery path of ardent need, tender desire, down her throat, pausing where her pulse leapt and jerked. She felt him smile against her skin.

Then he moved to her breast, taking his time, teasing her with his tongue, laughing softly at her arching gasp when he took her nipple into his mouth, and the shock of feeling was without fear, desire without shame.

The need he was creating within her was a thrumming pulse in her core, a glorious ache begging to be satisfied. And she knew he felt the same. Felt the pressure of his desire against her middle, heard his ragged gasp as he moved lower with his hands and his mouth.

'Alessandro…' It came out as a supplication as she lay there, subject, slave, to his devotions.

She tried to take control. She let her own hands drift lower, reaching for the pulsing heat of him. She saw his eyes darken with desire, heard his breathing hitch.

'*Mia gattina*…those claws are sharp!' He chuckled softly, capturing her hand with a groan. 'We have time…we have time…'

Meghan shook her head in protest. She didn't want to slow down. She didn't want to wait. She knew if she waited, if she let time and memory catch up to sensation, she would hesitate. She would start to doubt, to question, to fear.

To feel shame.

Now she just wanted to feel, feel *this*—his hands, his mouth, his body—with her senses and not her heart, to lose herself in the beauty and passion of being touched, caressed.

She wanted to feel…and to forget.

She knew that, and she pulled him to her to kiss him, hard, to banish the memories. The ghosts.

And then it stopped.

Alessandro pushed himself away from her, back onto his

knees. His face was flushed, his breathing ragged. He pulled a hand through his hair and exhaled slowly.

'We need to stop.'

Meghan stilled, stiffened in shock. Humiliation came—a fast, hot rush of feeling. She was suddenly conscious of how she must look, her hair in a tangle around her face, her lips swollen, cheeks flushed. Her shirt was hitched up around her neck, her bra clasp undone.

And Alessandro was looking at her with a quiet sorrow that made everything they'd just done seem dirty.

'Why?' She pulled her top down, and Alessandro stilled her hand.

'Don't. You're lovely.'

'You're not looking at me as if you're thinking that right now,' Meghan said, her voice coming out far more tremulous than she'd meant it to. 'What's wrong?'

'Nothing's wrong.' Alessandro stretched out beside her, tracing one finger along the tender skin of her navel. Meghan shuddered lightly.

'I'm rushing things,' he said after a moment. 'When we make love, it won't be like this.'

'Like what?'

'Rushed. Frenzied. Because we are angry.'

It took a great deal of her pride and courage to say, 'If I was angry, it was at myself. For wanting you.'

He paused, sitting up on one elbow to regard her thoughtfully. His fingers drifted up to touch her chin, tilting her face so their eyes met. He traced the outline of her lips with a fingertip.

'He hurt you very much, didn't he?'

Meghan opened her mouth soundlessly. She hadn't expected *that*. Hadn't expected tenderness on the heels of such passion, understanding coupled with desire. She nodded, helpless to deny what he already knew. 'Yes, he did.'

Undone by compassion where she'd expected condemnation, she felt tears sting her eyes. She forced them back. Lying next to him, her sorrow plain to see, Meghan felt far more exposed than when her clothes had been rucked up.

She tried to shrug away, but he stilled her with one gentle hand on her shoulder.

'Don't hide from me.'

'What do you want from me?' Meghan whispered. He wanted her body; she knew that. Understood it, even. Yet now he seemed to be asking for more. Her emotions, her desire, her soul.

Her heart.

Except he didn't want that, did he? He couldn't possibly want that.

Alessandro's eyes darkened even as he continued to stroke her face with tender, absent movements, a gesture of unthinking intimacy. 'I want you to want me,' he said at last. There was a hidden vulnerability in his voice that made Meghan ache.

Want him? Of course she wanted him. He had to know it. It was in her every look, her every word.

Her every thought.

'I do want you,' she admitted with a little laugh. 'I think that's obvious.'

'But you're ashamed,' Alessandro said quietly. 'Ashamed to be with me.' There was an ache in his voice, of need and pain, that Meghan couldn't begin to understand. It almost sounded as if he thought she were ashamed of *him*…rather than herself.

'I can't help that. I…I have a lot to get over, I suppose. When you touch me I want to forget. I want to feel and not to think.'

'That's only half of the experience.' He smiled down at her, his expression softened with tenderness, yet a shadow lingering in his eyes. 'You can make love with your body *and* your mind.'

'I suppose you're the expert?' Meghan said, and it came out halfway between a joke and a jibe.

'Perhaps with the body.' Alessandro's mouth tightened briefly before he smiled and brushed the hair back from her forehead, tangling his fingers in the silken strands. 'Like you, I'm waiting for my mind to catch up.'

Meghan's mouth opened soundlessly at this admission. *We're so alike.* Yet they were impossibly different. 'Where do we go from here?' she forced herself to ask, though at the moment she didn't want to know. She didn't want to leave. She didn't want Alessandro to leave.

She didn't know what she wanted.

'We wait.'

'For what?'

'For you to come to me of your own free will, with no shame, no fear, no frenzy. For both of us to give…completely.'

Meghan struggled to sit up, pushing her hair away from her face. Alessandro dropped his hand, still smiling.

'That's asking quite a lot.'

'I don't mind.'

'Maybe I do.'

He raised one eyebrow. 'Do you want to leave me?'

Meghan let out a shaky breath. 'No. But I should.'

'Why? What is this *should*?'

'Alessandro…' She closed her eyes, felt his fingers drift along her face. 'There's no future for us, is there? I'm not…'

'You're not what?'

She bit her lip. How could she explain her doubts, her fears, without opening the Pandora's box of her past? 'You thought I was a whore.' She hadn't meant to say it, didn't want to remind him, knew from the chilling silence that she shouldn't have. Her old wounds were too fresh, the scars raw and red.

Alessandro stiffened, his hand dropping from her face. Meghan opened her eyes.

He rolled off the bed, standing there, his chest brown and bare and glorious, his expression like iron.

'You still think I invited you here presuming you were a whore, that I hired you for a whore's work.' He shook his head, the movement sharp and contemptuous. 'This is old ground, Meghan. And I'm getting bored with it.'

'As you're bored with me?'

His voice was level, almost a drawl. 'Just about.'

Meghan swallowed painfully. He had the ability to hurt her so easily. 'But you judged me,' she whispered.

'Yes, I did. But you're the one judging *me* now.' There was a moment of taut silence, then Alessandro's hand slashed through the air. 'I won't have it, Meghan. I won't be judged—condemned on old evidence. I've had enough of that!' His voice was savage, yet as he turned away his head was bowed, as though under a burden too great to bear. 'I won't have you throwing one thing I said into my face time and time again,' he continued in a low voice. 'I *can't* have it. Nothing I ever say or do will prove what I am. You damn me on one piece of flimsy evidence. I will not be damned. Not by you.' His voice shook slightly. 'Not by you.'

Meghan stared, stunned by the force of his emotion. Her mind spun.

He turned back to her, his voice now cool. Cold. 'You must take responsibility for your own actions. Stop blaming me, or that other man, for your own desires. You may have been a victim before, but you are not one now. And I won't let you act like one.' He shook his head, his expression suddenly weary. 'There are too many shadows, Meghan. Perhaps for both of us. I'll drive you back to Spoleto, or wherever you want to go, tonight. It is better that way. It has to be.' With that, he gazed at her one last time, smiling sadly, then turned on his heel and left.

CHAPTER SIX

MEGHAN sat back on the bed, her mind still numb, yet whirling. Spinning horribly with implications she had pushed away, refused to consider.

You may have been a victim before, but you are not one now.

She lay back against the rumpled sheets and mussed pillows, an ache of regret throbbing through her, threatening to rise up into an overwhelming howl of misery.

She'd wanted control. She'd entered Alessandro's villa—his life—so she could prove something to herself. To him.

She'd wanted to prove that she was in control, that she wasn't a victim. She'd been determined to show how she could be in control of her own life, her own body.

She'd failed spectacularly.

She was such a fool.

She took a deep, shuddering breath. If she wanted control this was the time to take it with both hands, and show Alessandro she understood.

Meghan pushed the tangled mass of hair back from her flushed face. A glance in the mirror confirmed her suspicions; she was a mess. She splashed cold water on her face, yanked a brush through her hair until it lay in waves against her shoulders, and changed into a fresh pair of jeans from her haversack. She picked one of her favourite blouses, a silky, cream wraparound that emphasised the clean lines of her throat and collar-bone and left all the rest to the imagination, barely hinting at the soft curves it hid.

It was wrinkled and cheap, but it was clean, and it was hers. She didn't want to wear borrowed clothes for this.

Taking another breath, in a vain attempt to calm her wildly beating heart, she walked downstairs.

The villa was quiet, cloaked in darkness, but Meghan saw a lamp burning in the lounge. The double doors were closed, although one had escaped its latch.

It was enough of an invitation. It would have to be.

Meghan pushed the door open with her fingertips. Alessandro stood in the centre of the room, his back half turned, staring at one of the vivid oil paintings on the wall with a preoccupied scowl. When she saw the ferocity of his expression Meghan almost turned back.

Then he saw her. He stilled, then turned slightly towards her, one eyebrow raised, his face now frighteningly impassive, as if a mask had dropped into place. He didn't speak.

'I wanted to tell you I'm sorry,' Meghan began, her voice thready. 'You were right.'

'Oh?' He gave her nothing—no quarter, no mercy.

'I *was* acting like a victim,' Meghan continued painfully, her face flushing with humiliated acknowledgement, 'and it wasn't fair to you. Despite our…beginnings, you've given me nothing but honesty and understanding since then. I realise that now.' She swallowed, bowed her head in submission, and waited for his judgement.

Alessandro was silent. Meghan could hear her heart pounding.

'How convenient for you,' he said after a long moment, his voice dry, and yet with a chill.

'Alessandro, please.' Meghan looked up, took a step forward, reached a hand out in helpless appeal before dropping it. The man she'd thought she was beginning to know was warm, vibrant, alive.

The man in front of her now was a shadow of that man, no more than a reflection in ice.

He did not have compassion in his eyes. Tenderness did not soften his face. His eyes were black and cold, the beauty of his face made up only of harsh planes and angles.

'You really do want me to leave,' she said unsteadily.

He shrugged, an elegant twisting of his broad shoulders. 'Maybe you were right. Maybe I'm bored with you, as you suggested.'

Meghan felt sick. Alessandro was a man who didn't bluff. She should have known she'd wasted all her chances. She took a step backwards. 'I'll go and get my things.'

'Are you quite certain you want to return to Spoleto?' His expression was sardonic. 'You did say you were finished there.' He raised his eyebrows, coldly amused. 'So where are you going now, Meghan? Where are you running to? Have you decided that yet?'

'I'm not running,' Meghan retorted automatically, and Alessandro gave a sharp bark of laughter.

'Oh, no? But you give such a good impression of it.' He shook his head in disbelief. 'You're not a woman. You're a child. So young and naïve. You look to others to condemn or absolve you. You blame them for your mistakes—your choices—and you run away when it gets too hard. You have to take responsibility for your actions, Meghan. Lord knows I did—much as it hurt.'

Meghan jerked back from the verbal assault. He'd assessed and discarded her whole character in a matter of seconds. He'd given her reasons, motivations, faults, without understanding the truth.

Without knowing it.

'Don't,' she whispered. 'You don't know what you're talking about.'

'No? Then tell me.' Alessandro's face darkened even as he shoved his hands in his pockets, his body chillingly relaxed. 'Tell me about Stephen. He was married, you said? And you didn't know?'

Meghan's eyes widened in shock. 'No, I didn't! I told you that! He never told me...I never...'

'Yes, you've told me many things.' He made it sound as if she'd offered him a tissue of lies. 'This place you lived—Stanton Springs, was it? A small town? You told me you were—what was the phrase?—a smalltown girl.'

'Yes,' Meghan whispered wretchedly. 'It was a small place.' She knew where this was going, knew where he was leading her without mercy, without understanding. Without forgiveness. And she could do nothing but follow—follow down this damnable path to its terrible destination.

'I've heard about these towns in America. Friendly places, yes? Everyone knows everyone else. You all say hello in the street. Like one of those American television shows.' His eyes glinted with both knowledge and power.

'Yes,' Meghan agreed softly. 'It's just like that.'

He lifted his chin, prepared for the final thrust. 'So tell me now, how is it that you didn't know he was married? Because you *did* know, didn't you, Meghan?' His eyes were like blue flames, burning into hers, into her consciousness, her soul. Searing her. 'You must have known who he was. You must have said hello to his wife. You must have lived a lie. Isn't that right? That's what is eating you alive—why you have these shadows. Why you can't move on. You knew, and you pretended you didn't. Even to yourself. You knew, Meghan.'

It was too much—too close to the truth, and yet so horribly far from it. 'I didn't know!' Meghan shouted. Tears spurted from her eyes and her voice choked. 'I didn't know, it wasn't that small a town. He told me he was single! Damn you—damn you to hell, Alessandro di Agnio! I don't care what you say—what he said— I didn't know!'

He stilled, tensed. 'What did *he* say?'

'He said I should have known…that no one would believe I didn't know,' she choked out. The words, the confessions, tumbled from her lips. They'd been stamped down for so long, and now they couldn't come fast enough. 'He said everyone would assume I'd known—he was a model citizen, so was his wife. How could I not have known?'

'Indeed,' Alessandro said in a soft voice.

'But I didn't.' She was begging now, pleading for him to understand, to believe—as foolish a gesture as she knew that had to be. Who begged their accuser to understand? 'I didn't. I realise now how naïve I was. He was so charming, so…taken with me. I never stopped to question, to wonder why we always met in hotel rooms, seedy restaurants. I assumed he just wanted to keep a low profile because of his job. I thought it all so thrilling, but it's obvious now. Back then...then I was so starstruck, thinking myself so lucky, so in *love*, that I had no idea...no idea...' Her voice trailed off brokenly.

'No idea?' Alessandro prompted coolly.

'No idea of what I was getting into,' Meghan finished in a whisper. 'No idea what would happen. No idea that someone could think...'

'Think what?'

This was dangerous. Memories were dangerous. Her vision blurred and she clutched blindly at the chair. 'He thought I was nothing more than a whore,' she said, her voice so low that Alessandro leaned forward to hear. 'A whore,' she repeated disbelievingly. 'If you wonder why I thought that was what you meant by services, if you can't understand why it hurts so much that you thought that of me—even for a moment—then now you know.'

Alessandro regarded her quietly for a moment. 'Why would he think that?' he asked. 'Is there something you're not telling me?'

'He just did.' Meghan cut off a half-sob, took a shuddering breath. Her nerves were shattered, her emotions splintered. She felt as if Alessandro could sweep the broken pieces of her into his hand and blow them away. 'He just did, anyway.' Her voice came out dull, flat. She pressed her fist to her mouth, bit down on her knuckles. Hard. She couldn't say more. She couldn't tell him any more.

'And you started to believe it?' he surmised thoughtfully.

Meghan swung round to face him, horrified. 'No, of course I didn't! I would never—!'

'Yes, you did,' Alessandro countered softly. 'You've believed it all this time, haven't you? You think it was your fault. And you've never forgiven yourself.'

'*What*?' She jerked back as if she'd been slapped. 'Forgive myself? You think I need that?' She shook her head so hard her hair tangled against her face, and she brushed it away in one angry, impatient gesture. 'I forgave myself a long time ago—if there was anything to forgive. *Which there wasn't.*' Her breathing hitched and she forced herself to sound calm.

There was no truth in what Alessandro was saying. There

was no *sense*. Could he actually think she was to blame for what had happened? For what she hadn't *known*? For what had happened next…?

'Perhaps there wasn't anything to forgive,' Alessandro agreed evenly. 'But you blamed yourself all the same, didn't you? You tell me now you didn't know. But maybe there was a little whisper in your heart. Deep down you thought, you must have known. You must have at least suspected.'

Meghan stared at him transfixed. Horrified. She felt stripped bare…again. This time more vulnerable than ever before, and it hurt. It hurt so much. More than physical blows. Still, she could not look away from Alessandro's gaze, his eyes blazing with knowledge. Knowledge of her heart, her mind.

'Maybe I did,' she whispered, the words torn from her.

'That's why you thought I was propositioning you outside the restaurant.'

'You were—'

'No. I told you. Richard Harrison—the man here earlier— wanted to proposition you.' Alessandro's lips curled in distaste. 'I wanted no part in that plan.'

'You still thought—'

'Yes.' He held up a hand, cutting her off. 'Until you told me I was talking to the wrong kind of woman.' He smiled sadly, spreading his hands wide. 'It stunned me at first. But what kind of woman assumes she's being propositioned that way? Not a true whore—because that kind of woman would take it in her stride, sidle up to me and make an offer. Another woman—most women—would ask me what I meant, perhaps, or assume that since I'd called you out of the restaurant I naturally wanted your services as a waitress. But you didn't. And it made me wonder.'

Meghan swallowed. Her throat was dry, as if it were coated in sandpaper. 'What did it make you wonder?' she whispered huskily.

'It made me wonder why you thought you were a whore when you so obviously weren't. That's why you flirted that way, isn't it? Why you stayed at that hostel—why you never reported Paulo. Why you keep thinking I'm treating you like one, thinking of you as one. Because you think you deserve it.'

Meghan shook her head. 'I don't deserve it.' Her voice broke, and she couldn't keep the tears from clogging her throat, her eyes. She blinked them back; they fell anyway, tracing silver tracks down her face. 'I *don't*.'

Wordlessly Alessandro put his arms around her, drawing her to him. Meghan let herself be pulled against him, let him tuck her chin against his chest.

He couldn't see her face, yet his thumb still traced her cheek, wiping away the tear that slipped softly, silently down—as if he'd followed its track with his heart. He was holding her as close as a lover, as gently as a child.

'*Mia gattina*, of course you don't. Of course. I know that. Perhaps you know it in your mind, but not in your heart. Where it matters.'

She closed her eyes. For a long moment there was nothing but the sound of their own ragged breathing. Alessandro stroked her hair softly.

'What…what happens now?' Meghan asked in little more than a whisper.

Alessandro tensed, then sighed, a shuddering breath that made Meghan realise he was not as much in control as she'd thought. She'd been laid bare, but somehow, in some way, so had he.

He understood.

Why? How?

'What happens now?' Alessandro repeated almost musingly. She felt rather than saw his smile. 'Now you marry me.'

The silence in the room was deafening, a roaring in her ears. Meghan froze, then forced herself to move away. She stared at him, looking for humour, for mockery. For something to tell her he was not, could not possibly be, serious. There was nothing in his face to indicate he was joking. He looked bland, impassive, yet Meghan suspected that blank look was his brand of armour. What did that mask hide? What emotions? What hopes?

Marriage?

Meghan shook her head.

'You're joking.'

'Do you really think I would joke about marriage?'

She shook her head slowly, hating the sudden flare of hope and need that he had ignited within her. 'Why would you want to marry me?'

'Just because you think so little of yourself doesn't mean I do.'

'You just acted like you thought very little of me indeed,' Meghan said through stiff, numb lips. 'You called me a child, you blamed me for what happened—'

'I drove you to confession,' Alessandro corrected quietly. 'Absolution.'

'Oh, is that what that was?' Meghan slapped her forehead in a parody of understanding. 'Sorry. Silly me. Because it sure didn't feel that way. It felt like you were condemning me for every single thing I thought you didn't believe!'

'I don't,' Alessandro said calmly. 'Not now. But I knew you did, and I had to show you that. Only then would you be able to move on. Stop blaming, stop being the victim.'

'Thanks for the psychotherapy.' Meghan turned away in disgust—disgust at herself for falling into his trap, and for the damn thing *working*.

He knew her better than she knew herself, and it didn't make sense. It wasn't fair. She didn't like feeling so vulnerable, so exposed, so *raw*.

And yet, she realised with sudden, sweet surprise, it was a relief.

It was a relief to be known and not judged. To be accepted, not condemned. To not carry the burden of her secrets, her shame, alone.

'Marry me, Meghan.'

It was tempting. Far, far too tempting. To marry a man she barely knew, a man she shouldn't trust.

Except she did trust him. More, she knew, than she'd ever trusted anyone else.

'Alessandro, it's crazy.' She tried to laugh; it came out as a wobble. 'We barely know each other.'

'Actually, I think I know you rather well.'

That much was true. How had he slipped beneath her defences, her *skin*? When had it happened? How had she not seen, felt, realised until now, when she was exposed and empty and he was tempting her with promises, with hope?

With a second chance.

'I don't know you,' Meghan pointed out. That was true, too. She didn't understand him at all—couldn't fathom how such tenderness could be coupled with a refusal to love, how his smiles hid a seething darkness, a vulnerable need so at odds with the strength and control he radiated.

'You know you can trust me, at least. Don't you?'

'Yes…' She just didn't know where that trust would lead her.

'So why not?'

'*Why*? Why not an affair? A few days at your villa and then a sweet parting? Isn't that what you had in mind all along?' Her chin lifted in challenge even as the words rent her soul.

Alessandro raised his eyebrows. 'Is that all you think you're worth? An affair? Not marriage?'

'I thought *you* thought that was all I was worth,' Meghan responded quietly.

He inclined his head in cool acknowledgement. 'Now you know that's not true.'

Meghan tried to laugh, to pierce the unreality of the situation. 'You haven't fallen in love with me, have you?' She'd meant it as a joke, but it fell horribly flat. It came out as a plea, a prayer.

'No,' he said slowly. 'But then you haven't fallen in love with me either. We don't believe in love, remember? Or was that a lie?' His expression turned hard for a moment.

She looked away, out of the window. Twilight was descending on the hills with a purple softness, a peace was cloaking the world that felt so removed from the shattered atmosphere of this room.

'No, it wasn't a lie.' She'd loved Stephen, and he'd used it to his advantage, to control her, time and time again. She'd accepted the snubs, the sneaking around, the hasty moments and couplings, because she'd thought that was what you did when you loved someone. You accepted whatever they gave. You gave whatever they were willing to take.

No matter how much it hurt. No matter how much it cost.

'Good.'

She looked at him curiously. How could such a gentle and tender man be so hard, so unforgiving? 'Have you ever been in love?'

'No.'

'Never? And you never want to be?'

'No. Love is a cheap emotion, used to manipulate and blame. I'm not interested in love.'

'You've loved *someone*, surely?'

Alessandro's mouth twisted in a bitter smile. 'My heart's not broken, if that's what you mean.'

Meghan shook her head. 'There must be some reason why you don't want to love…be loved. It's a natural human desire. You know my reason. What's yours?'

His eyes narrowed, blackened. 'Don't analyse me, Meghan. Don't try. Just understand this. I won't love you. Ever. And I won't be loved.' His voice tightened ominously. 'And, Meghan, if you think you can make me change my mind, you can't. I don't love. Anybody. Not even my mother, my father. Not you. You should know that from the start. I thought, in fact, that such a…condition might appeal to you. No danger—isn't that right?' He smiled mockingly. 'Our hearts don't need to be involved. *Won't* be involved.'

She would have had to have been deaf not to hear the warning. 'But why should I marry you?' she protested, hating how weak her voice sounded.

His smile was lethal, predatory, possessing. 'You desire me. It is a good basis for marriage.'

'Physical desire?' Meghan didn't bother keeping the disbelief from her voice. 'Sex?'

He shrugged, unperturbed. 'Why not? If we were married there would be no shame in that.' His gaze roamed over her again.

Meghan felt a blush stain the tender skin between her breasts, crawl up her throat. She watched Alessandro watch that humiliating, revealing stain, a smile playing about his lips. He stared at her, his expression smouldering, daring her to respond, to deny what pulsated between them.

'A high price for you to pay to sleep with me,' Meghan couldn't help but jibe, and Alessandro slashed his hand through the air.

'Do not debase yourself to me. Ever.' He paused, his words

becoming a caress, a temptation. 'You would have security, Meghan. No more waitressing, no more grotty hostels. No more running.'

'I don't need you for that,' she whispered.

'No, but it would help, wouldn't it? What about when you go back home?'

'I'm not going back home!'

'Not now,' Alessandro agreed, his tone far too placid, too convincing. 'But never? Can you honestly say you will never see your family again?'

Meghan swallowed. 'I don't know.'

'If you are married to me you can go home with your head held high, a husband at your side. A rather powerful husband. I could buy out all the poky little shops in that town if you wanted me to.'

Meghan managed a shaky laugh. 'I'm not interested in revenge.'

'I'm not talking about revenge. I'm talking about power. Power that won't be abused. Power that you will have at your disposal. The power not to be ashamed. Afraid.'

Colour scorched her cheeks once more. Alessandro caught her hand in his, stroked the tender skin of her palm.

'Can you tell me you don't want that?' he asked softly. 'Can you tell me that isn't tempting to you?'

Meghan looked down. His finger stroked her palm, her wrist, her heart. How did he know? How could he possibly guess the thoughts racing through her mind so easily?

Power. The thought called to her with a siren song, lured her forward to a treacherous future. She could be secure. She could live without fear. Safe from the past, the knowing looks, the scorching shame.

She couldn't wander her way through Europe for ever; it was a half-life at best. She'd put off thinking of the future because she was afraid to face it.

She knew she could start over in another town, begin another life, but the prospect held no appeal. The shame would still be there—the fear that someone would believe what Stephen had, would act as Stephen had.

With Alessandro as her husband she would never need to be

afraid again. She would be in control…with him. She could hold her head high.

She could finally have power, and it would not be abused.

She shook her head. It was crazy, but it was tempting.

'And what do you get out of this bargain?' she asked after a moment, uneasy suspicion rippling through her.

'I get a wife who won't expect me to love her. A wife I desire. Most women want to marry for love. I'm not interested in deceiving or disappointing them. The women who don't want to marry for love are usually after money. Mine. I'm not interested in them either.'

It sounded chilling, as soulless as a business transaction at a bank. 'If you're so against love,' Meghan asked quietly, 'why marry at all?'

He hunched one shoulder in a half-shrug. 'I told you before. It's not easy being alone.'

'Get a dog,' she snapped, and he smiled faintly.

'I don't want a dog.'

'What *do* you want, Alessandro?' Meghan asked, and she held her breath for the answer.

His expression stilled, blanked. Although his face was a mask, she sensed the urgency underneath. 'I want you.'

Meghan's heart lurched. Yearned. This was what she wanted to hear. Yet she was still afraid. She couldn't trust it. Not this time. Not again. 'Why me?'

'I don't know,' he admitted, with an honesty that stung just a little. 'But I want you, Meghan. I want a life…a life that's different. A life together.'

'But without love?' Meghan clarified, after her heart had stopped stumbling. 'It sounds kind of cold.'

'It doesn't have to be.'

'Tell me how.'

'Companionship, desire, affection.' He ticked them off on his fingers. 'Don't those mean something to you?'

All too much. 'What's the difference?' Meghan challenged. 'Wouldn't you call those things love?'

He levelled her with one knowing look. 'Would you?'

No. Love was needing someone like air or water. Needing

despite the desire or affection. Needing even though it hurt, even though pain sliced through you, even though it killed you.

She glanced away. 'What about children?' There was an ache of longing like a physical pain, deep in her belly.

'Do I want them? Yes. I need an heir. Someone to run Di Agnio Enterprises when I am gone. Someone to pass it on to.'

'And would you love your children?' Meghan asked, her throat raw and aching.

Alessandro paused. 'I would certainly give them every affection, every opportunity.'

Meghan shook her head. Was it possible to have affection and desire—to enjoy them—without love? She didn't know. Didn't know if she could take the risk to find out.

His hand circled her wrist and he pulled her towards him, caressing her with his words. 'You can stop running, Meghan. You can stop hiding who you are, what happened to you. I already know, and I accept you. I believe you. Does it really matter if I don't love you?'

She was so near she could feel his breath feathering her face. She lifted her head, saw the truth, the heat blazing in his eyes.

She was tired of running. Of being alone, afraid, ashamed.

'I wasn't looking to be rescued,' she said in a low voice.

He smiled, skimming his fingers along her cheek. 'We never are.'

'And you? Will I be enough for you?' Meghan asked, a thread of uncertainty, of fear, in her voice. 'What if you get tired of being married? Being married to me? What then?'

Alessandro looked down at her, blinked slowly as he took in her words. When he spoke his voice was quiet, yet as strong and taut as a wire. 'I honour my promises,' he said. 'I honour my word. No matter what you…or anyone…thinks. That is the man I am. The man I mean to be.' He spoke with a fierce determination that roughened his tone and burned in his eyes.

She wanted to believe. She wanted to so much.

'It can happen,' he promised softly. 'It can happen for both of us. We can forget the past, what people thought, what they believed. We can be something new—something wonderful and true—to each other.'

It sounded wonderful. But was it real? And could it happen without love? And what was *he* running from?

'I…I need to think about it,' she said, her voice a raw whisper. 'It's too big a decision to make so quickly.'

'I can give you tonight,' Alessandro said. 'Tomorrow I have to return to Milan, to deal with business. Insulting Richard Harrison—as satisfying as it was—is sure to have repercussions.'

'And if I say no in the morning?' Meghan asked, transfixed by the unreality of the situation.

'I'll take you to the station in Spoleto. Or the airport—wherever you'd like to go.'

A ticket to her next destination. The thought had no appeal. Her travelling, once exciting and vibrant, was now just another excuse to run away.

Yet the realisation that he would dismiss her so easily—so coldly—chilled her to the marrow.

'And if I say yes?' she whispered.

'You come with me to Milan, meet my family, and we get married.'

Alessandro spread his hands, smiling, although there was a coolness, a remoteness in his eyes that stung Meghan's soul. Who was this man? Would she ever understand him?

'As soon as possible.'

'That easy?' she asked, in both disbelief and hope.

'That easy.'

The sky was inky black, studded with stars, as Alessandro prowled along the terrace outside. He'd already knocked back a glass of whisky, the fiery liquid burning all the way to his gut, and it hadn't helped.

What had he done?

He'd asked Meghan Selby—a virtual stranger—to marry him. A pretty young woman he'd mistaken for a whore—who'd mistaken *herself* for a whore.

He laughed aloud—a rasping sound that echoed in the still night and held no humour.

He didn't think Meghan was a whore. She was, he thought

with something close to regret, far too innocent. Too naïve...
about him.

He recalled the aching vulnerability in her eyes, the shadows
of both remembered and anticipated pain, and cursed himself—
not for a fool, but for a madman.

A devil.

What kind of a man but a devil offered marriage to a woman
who had been so badly hurt—who surely deserved only love and
tenderness when he could offer her neither?

He could pretend to be tender. He could say the right words,
do the right things. Because he knew what the response would
be, the response he wanted.

He knew how to play her.

He was good at that. He'd always been good at that.

Alessandro raked a hand through his hair and cursed softly.
He'd finished with hurting people, with acting selfishly and
leaving ruin and grief in his wake.

That was his old life. He'd put it aside two years ago, along
with the memory of a smoking ruin and the still, lifeless form of
his older brother.

And yet now he was risking not only his own soul—which
he'd long since condemned—but someone else's.

Meghan's.

A woman who deserved so, so much more than he could give.

A woman who deserved so much more than him.

He stared out at the midnight sky, at the sliver of moon, pale
and luminous, suspended above a still world, silent save for the
rustling of leaves in the olive trees.

Eyes like sunlight on an olive grove.

Why had he asked her to marry him?

She would have agreed to an affair. He could have worked her
out of his system, left her at the train station with a diamond
bracelet and no backward glances.

He'd done it before. Many times.

So why marriage? Why now? Why her?

*Because I'm not that man any more. I don't want to be that
man any more.*

His lips twisted into a smile—a smile of self-loathing and also of self-acknowledgement.

He *was* that man. That wouldn't change. He could pose, he could pretend, but underneath ultimately he knew who he was. Everyone knew who he was.

Everyone but Meghan.

He wasn't like her—judged, condemned falsely by one twisted man. He'd been condemned by the truth.

The truth of who he was.

And yet…he wanted her. Wanted her with a desire that shook him, paralysed him with its blinding need, its power. Even made him a little bit afraid.

He wanted a saviour.

The realisation made him hurl his whisky tumbler onto the paving stones, where it shattered. Some things couldn't be fixed.

Not the tumbler. Not him.

He was past redemption, past saving. He knew that; he'd been told it many times. He saw it in his own soul and he accepted the truth, as everyone who knew him had accepted it.

No matter how hard he tried, how far he ran, it wouldn't change.

He couldn't change.

She could change me.

It was a joke; it wasn't fair. He couldn't expect Meghan to save him, love him. Didn't want it.

Didn't want to need it.

He didn't want—*shouldn't* want—some pathetic, needy smalltown girl trying to fix him. Trying to love him. No matter what she said, he knew she would start to love him. He saw it in her eyes—the hope and the fear.

I won't love…or be loved.

Except she had eyes like sunlight, and when she smiled he felt…hope.

But there was no hope, could be no hope. Not for him.

He was damned.

If he married Meghan he would be dragging her down with him. Taking her with him to hell.

But he still wanted her. And he would have her. No matter what it took. No matter what it cost.

Because, Alessandro acknowledged with a bitter, mocking toast to himself, that was the kind of man he was. He was a selfish bastard who took his pleasures where he could, how he could, no matter who he hurt.

And he would hurt Meghan. He might try not to for a while, but the truth would out.

His own nature would out.

No matter what he'd tried to prove in the last two years, the reality was his own blackened soul...and what it would do to Meghan.

Hating himself, Alessandro turned back inside.

CHAPTER SEVEN

MEGHAN awoke to sunlight washing the room in shades of yellow and cream, a slight breeze from the open window ruffling the curtains.

She leaned her head against the pillow, willing herself to enjoy the simple sensual pleasure of the moment before the thoughts, the memories, the doubts came rushing back in.

And so they came, hurtling through her mind with stunning force, leaving her breathless when she hadn't even moved.

She'd almost made love with Alessandro.

He'd stripped her bare, taken away her pretences, her pride.

He'd asked her to marry him.

Meghan pressed her fists to her eyes, wanting to cry, needing the release, but she'd already shed all her tears.

Her eyes were dry and gritty. It had been a long, sleepless night. Yet now, despite the agony of remembering, of allowing herself to process all that had happened, she realised she felt calm.

She felt strong.

She sat up in bed, pushing her hair away from her face. Today was a new day. Today was the beginning of a new life.

Last night, somewhere between midnight and dawn, she'd decided to marry Alessandro.

It had been a long night of doubt, of uncertainty, and yet also of hope. Her mind told her to run far, far away from Villa Tre Querce, from the hold Alessandro had on her.

And yet she also knew she would never be able to run far

enough. In the space of a few days he'd already marked her heart, her mind, her soul.

Even her body.

Just the thought of his hands on her, his fingers lightly skimming her skin, made her shiver in remembered pleasure.

I want you to touch me.

She drew her knees up, resting her chin on top. The breeze blowing from the window was warm, a sign of oncoming summer.

A new life.

What would life be like with Alessandro? The question sent a delicious shiver of anticipation through her, yet chasing it was the sharp bite of fear.

It could all go so horribly, horribly wrong.

Meghan closed her eyes as doubt assailed her once more.

Why was she doing this? It would be easier, safer to run away. Find a new place since she couldn't return home.

Home. Just the word—the concept—brought pain slicing through her as a grim smile twisted her features.

You knew. You wanted it. You deserved it.

The voices of the past, still haunting her. The shadows, she realised, still there.

Would they ever go away?

You haven't told him the truth.

The treacherous whisper of her conscience made her shudder. She could not tell Alessandro the truth. She could not share with him the extent of her shame. Admittedly it was hard for him to believe that she would think so little of herself simply because she hadn't known Stephen was married.

If he knew how low she'd been brought...how ashamed she'd been...

The shadows flickered about the room, the echoes of Stephen's taunts and leers like whispers in the corners.

And now? Wasn't she just opening herself to the possibility of even more pain, more humiliation than ever before?

Yes, Meghan thought. She was.

Except now the power would be on her side. She would never

be helpless again, never a pawn in someone else's filthy desire, disgusting needs. She would never again be a victim.

Unless she was Alessandro's.

The thought chilled her. If she fell in love with him, if she let him inside her heart even just a tiny bit, it could hurt.

It could hurt so much.

But that was a risk she was going to have to take.

When she'd run out of Stanton Springs she'd also run out of choices. She couldn't go home. She couldn't keep running. Not for ever.

Alessandro had been right when he'd asked, 'Does it really matter if I don't love you?'

Even though the question had caused her pain, she recognised the truth. It didn't matter. It couldn't.

She didn't want to love him; he wouldn't love her.

They could still be happy. And she would have power. Control. At last.

Why wouldn't he love anyone? What was his secret? The truth behind the need?

That is the man I am. The man I mean to be.

If it were within her power she would help him become that man. She would make it happen.

Maybe one day he would tell her. And maybe, Meghan thought grimly, she would tell him. The truth. The whole truth.

Maybe.

Her stomach churning with nerves, but also with a new, fiery determination, she sprang out of bed. She dressed in her own clothes—faded jeans and a butter-yellow jumper. She pinned her hair back carelessly on top of her head and scanned her reflection in the mirror. She was pale, too pale, and her eyes looked huge, but there were freckles on her nose from the sun yesterday, and she couldn't quite contain the smile lurking underneath her fear.

Dragging a shaky breath into her lungs, she headed downstairs. The house was silent, waiting, as Meghan descended the sweeping staircase, one hand on the wrought-iron railing.

Was Ana back? How would the taciturn housekeeper respond

to the news that her employer was marrying? That he was marrying Meghan?

Meghan took another breath. She needed air.

She found Alessandro in the kitchen, drinking coffee and reading the newspaper as if he hadn't a care in the world. His head was bent and his hair fell boyishly over his forehead. He raked it back with one careless hand, absorbed in the paper.

Meghan's heart felt as if it had been squeezed, as if Alessandro had reached right inside and tugged even when he'd barely moved. Even when he hadn't seen her.

Ana stood at the stove, preparing breakfast. She flashed Meghan a quick, malevolent glance before her face went blank and she turned back to the eggs on her stove.

Meghan shifted uneasily. She had an enemy there, and she didn't even know why.

'Alessandro?'

He turned quickly, smiling easily, although Meghan could see the shadows in his eyes. Something was troubling him, and she wasn't sure if it was her.

'*Buongiorno*. Did you sleep well?'

Meghan laughed dryly. 'Not really.'

'No?' Alessandro shrugged, spreading his hands. 'You had a lot to think about, I suppose.'

'Maybe I'd already made my decision,' Meghan retorted, nettled a bit by his arrogance.

'Maybe you had.'

He looked so calm, so urbane, dressed in pale cream trousers with a leather belt, a light green button-down shirt open at the throat, scuffed yet exquisitely made leather loafers on his feet. His hair was still damp and curly from the shower.

'What do you think it was?' Meghan couldn't resist asking. She folded her arms, staring him down.

Alessandro chuckled. 'Meghan, I don't *think* what it was. I know.'

'Oh?' She was half inclined to tell him she wouldn't marry him now. He didn't have to look so certain!

'You'd made up your mind before I had even left the room,'

Alessandro continued. The smugness was gone, replaced by simple soft honesty. 'And if you hadn't, it didn't matter. Because I'd made up mine.'

'You can't force me to marry you!'

'Who said anything about force?' His eyes had darkened dangerously, and Meghan felt her pulse thrum in response. It didn't take much to have her swaying into him, longing for his look, his touch.

She was conscious of Ana behind them, pots and pans clanking ominously as she moved around the kitchen.

He reached for her hand, pulling her to him slowly, even though she made a pretence of resisting. When she stood only inches away, their bodies still not touching, he brushed his lips against her palm.

'You look beautiful like that—so natural, so unaffected.'

Meghan looked up, startled. 'Sloppy, more like.'

'No.' Alessandro touched her cheek, trailing his fingers down to gently grasp her chin. 'I meant what I said. You're beautiful.'

'Thank you,' Meghan whispered. 'You're beautiful too.'

Alessandro smiled, and she saw it reached his eyes.

'And you'll marry me.'

She wanted to argue, to deny it simply to resist his autocratic dictates, but she couldn't. It was true, and she wanted it to be true.

I can make you happy, she thought.

'Yes.'

Alessandro's smile deepened, and she saw a new satisfaction there, deeper than any she'd seen before. A hunger satisfied.

'Thank you,' he said simply, humbly, accepting her acceptance as a gift, a treasure. Meghan's heart ached.

I can make you happy. Give me a chance. Even if there's no love. The words buzzed in her mind. She almost said them, gulping them back, choking on air.

Alessandro smiled. 'Let's eat.'

Over breakfast, with Ana serving in courteous if rather stony silence, Alessandro informed Meghan of their plans.

'We must leave for Milan after breakfast. I have business to attend to, and I want to introduce you to my family. The sooner they know you, the sooner we can get married.' His expression darkened briefly before he turned brisk and businesslike again.

'Why does it have to be so quick?' Meghan asked. Her mind was spinning and she took a steadying sip of coffee. 'We could take time to get to know each other. Be sure we're not making a mistake.'

'I'm not making a mistake,' Alessandro replied with easy confidence. 'And I want to marry quickly because I want you in my bed every night.'

Meghan flushed. 'And we need to be married for that?'

He paused, his lips twitching. 'You do. I won't have you feeling guilty or ashamed about what happens between us. Ever.'

Meghan was conscious of Ana clearing their dishes. She didn't think the housekeeper understood much English, yet surely Alessandro's intimate caressing tone came across in any language?

'Thank you for that respect,' she managed stiffly.

Ana loaded the dishwasher while they finished their coffee, and then retreated to another part of the house. Meghan watched her broad back disappear with a twitch of unease.

'She doesn't like me,' she said suddenly.

Alessandro glanced up from the newspaper headlines he'd been scanning once more. 'Who? Ana?'

'Yes, she disapproves of me. I can tell. She glared at me when I came into the kitchen.' Meghan toyed with the handle of her coffee mug. 'Is it always going to be like that?'

'Not when we are married,' Alessandro replied in a flat, final tone. 'And you'll discover that Ana doesn't disapprove of you. She disapproves of me.'

Meghan looked up in surprise, but Alessandro had moved on. He swept the newspaper aside with unconcern and smiled.

'There are other matters to attend to in Milan. You will need clothes—that haversack cannot hold much. I have a flat in Milan, but perhaps you would like to live somewhere new? I leave such decisions to you.'

'I'm sure the flat you have now is fine,' Meghan said faintly. She was reeling from the barrage of information. What was she actually going to *do* in Milan, in her new life?

'You know, I was a teacher in Stanton Springs,' she said hesitantly. 'Languages. I quit my job when…'

'A teacher?' Alessandro glanced at her swiftly, assessingly.

'Well, of course if you want to teach again in Milan I have no problem with it. Perhaps at one of the English or American schools? Something part-time, so you can travel with me if needed?' His voice lowered, filled with promise. 'I don't want to leave you alone…or to be alone myself.'

She nodded. 'Yes…part-time. I'll look into it.'

'*Buon*. But first my family, and the wedding.'

The thought of meeting other di Agnios sent a stab of fear through her. Taking another sip of coffee to quell the nerves rising queasily upwards, Meghan asked, 'What exactly is your business? You mentioned the jewellery boutiques, the property and the finance, but are there other things as well?'

'My grandfather started with the jewels. My father chose to branch out into property, electronics, shipping.' He shrugged. 'A piece of every pie. The jewellery, of course, is our flagship enterprise—what we are truly known for.' He drummed his fingers on the table. 'The man you met yesterday, as unpleasant as he was, owns one of the largest chains of department stores in the United States. We were negotiating a contract to feature Di Agnio jewels in select stores—our own boutique within the department store, as it were.' He shrugged. 'It's no matter.'

'It sounds like quite a big business deal,' Meghan said after a moment.

'There are other deals,' Alessandro replied in dismissal. 'And no deal, business or otherwise, is worth making if you lose your self-respect.'

'Is that what we're making?' Meghan asked suddenly. Her hands tightened on her coffee mug. 'A business deal?'

Alessandro frowned. 'Marriage is a contract, certainly,' he replied. 'But I do not consider it business.' His eyes narrowed. 'Having second thoughts, *cara*?'

'What if I was?'

'I would tell you it is too late. We drive to Milan within the hour.'

'Too late?' Meghan echoed incredulously. 'Are you always going to be this bossy, Alessandro? Because I won't have you ordering me around—'

In response, Alessandro plucked the coffee cup from her

fingers and set it on the table. 'Go and get ready. I've just decided I want to leave as soon as possible.'

'You mean,' Meghan retorted, 'you want to stop this conversation.'

'As a matter of fact, yes. Why don't you pack your things? It won't take long.'

Wordlessly Meghan rose from the table. She wasn't going to waste her energy or emotions on arguing over such petty things. She knew she'd need to save them for later—for the bigger, more important battles that were sure to come.

She went upstairs. Stuffed her few paltry possessions into the worn haversack.

'What am I doing?' she muttered, a bubble of hysteria rising inside her, threatening to escape in a wild peal of laughter. 'What am I *doing*?'

She was leaving for Milan to meet the di Agnio family…to be introduced as Alessandro's fiancée. Bride.

It was so crazy. It was so real. She didn't know what to do but continue to move forward, one inch at a time. If she looked further than the next day, the next moment, she would fall into an abyss of fear and doubt.

'I washed your things.' Ana stood in the doorway, her expression close to a glare. Meghan's waitressing uniform was folded neatly in her hands.

'Thank you, Ana,' she replied in Italian.

Meghan took the clothes hesitantly. Disapproval and dislike rolled from the woman in waves, and she felt compelled to say something.

'You know I am marrying Signor di Agnio?' she said, and Ana nodded stiffly.

'You will—' she began, struggling to find the words. 'You will make him happy?' It was as much an order as a request.

Meghan blinked in surprise. 'He told me you didn't like him,' she blurted out.

'I don't like the man he has become. The boy he was…here…I loved.' Ana blinked and shrugged, impatient. 'Goodbye, *signorina*.'

She left the room, and Meghan stuffed the clothes into her haversack, her mind whirling.

The man he has become.

The man I mean to be.

What was the difference?

'Ready?' Alessandro asked from the doorway. He'd shrugged on a beautifully tailored jacket, worn with unselfconscious ease and grace. 'It takes about two hours to drive to Milan. We'll go straight to my mother's house, if you don't mind.'

With the sunshine turning the distant green fields to gold, Meghan watched the Villa Tre Querce disappear as they drove down the steep, winding hill and through the wrought-iron gates.

'When will we be back?' she asked after a moment.

Alessandro glanced at her. 'To the villa? Who knows? We can plan a honeymoon, of course. Somewhere different…somewhere neither of us have ever been.'

Meghan regarded him thoughtfully. It almost sounded as if she were not the only one who was used to running away.

What are your secrets? she wanted to ask. *What are you hiding from me?* She could hardly ask for the truth now, when she was hiding so much herself. There was time. There had to be time.

Neither of them spoke as Alessandro drove past Spoleto into Tuscany. The fields on either side of the motorway were a blur of browns and greens, and Meghan leaned back in her seat and closed her eyes.

She was, she realised, completely exhausted. She must have dozed, for she woke up as the car began to climb the foothills into Lombardy. Alessandro smiled at her as she sat up, shrugging strands of hair from her eyes.

'We're about an hour away. I've telephoned my mother. She expects us for lunch.'

'Great.' Meghan swallowed nervously. 'Maybe you could tell me about your family?'

He shrugged. 'There is not much to know. My mother, Gabriella, lives in the house I was born in—in Milan. My father died four years ago of a heart attack. My sister, Chiara, lives in London. She works for Di Agnio Enterprises there.'

'And your brother?'

He pressed his lips together, shook his head. 'I told you before. He is dead.'

'Right. I'm sorry.' Meghan felt as if every word she spoke was prodding a nest of vipers, full of poisonous secrets. 'When did he die?'

'Two years ago.'

'Was it from a disease?'

'Car accident.' He spoke so tightly that Meghan almost didn't hear the bitten-out words.

'And what about his wife…?'

'She lives in Rome. You'll find Paula will have nothing to do with me. With us. We needn't consider her at all.' Alessandro spoke so dispassionately, so coldly, that Meghan knew it was a subject she must drop.

For now.

'So I'm just meeting your mother today?' That was easier than a houseful of faceless disapproving di Agnios. One woman she hoped she could handle.

'Yes. Chiara, I hope, will fly to Milan for the wedding.' He glanced at her enquiringly. 'That is, if you agree to a wedding in Milan? Naturally I assumed you did not wish to return to Stanton Springs.'

'Naturally.' Meghan felt the beginnings of a headache. She massaged her temples. 'A wedding in Milan is fine. Something small.'

'Of course. Small, but tasteful.' His mouth quirked in a smile. 'Elegant. Do you wish to notify your family? Perhaps there is someone—a friend—you would like to attend?'

Meghan thought of her family—her two older sisters, safely married and quick to judge, the disapproval and disappointment of her parents who hadn't been able to understand how it had come to this. As for friends—Stephen had pushed them all away, and now she was too embarrassed to tell them the truth.

No one wanted to hear a truth like this. Not in a small town.

'No,' she said after a moment, her voice a thread of sound. 'There's no one.'

Alessandro's mouth tightened, but he did not insult her with pity. 'Just as well. Everything will be easier to arrange.'

The fields and foothills gave way to houses as they entered Milan. On the horizon Meghan saw a cluster of skyscrapers bearing silent witness to the fact that Milan was one of the most glamorous and cosmopolitan cities in Europe.

'Will…will your mother like me, do you think?' Meghan asked, trying to keep her voice diffident.

Alessandro laughed once—a sharp, bitter sound. 'Don't waste your time trying to make people like you, Meghan.'

She blinked. 'But, Alessandro, this is your mother. Of course I want her to like me.'

'Why? She doesn't like *me*.' He stared straight ahead, his expression grim.

'Is that why you don't love her?' Meghan asked after a moment.

'No. I don't love her because I don't love anyone.' Alessandro flexed his hands on the steering wheel as he navigated the increasing city traffic. 'You're not thinking you can change me, Meghan, are you?' he said, his voice pleasant but with the hint of a warning. 'Because I told you once before—you can't. Don't make the mistake of entering this marriage thinking you can change me, save me.'

Save me. The words echoed through Meghan's mind. Did she think she could save Alessandro? Make him believe in love?

No, surely not. Surely she wasn't that desperately naïve. Besides, Meghan thought, you couldn't save anyone. You could only believe they were worth saving.

Did Alessandro think he needed saving? Didn't he think he was worth it? The questions buzzed round in her brain with no answers.

Meghan stared straight ahead. The gothic spires of Il Duomo rose in the distance, as elegant and ostentatious as the decorations on a wedding cake.

'No,' she said flatly. 'I'm not that foolish.'

'Good.'

She glanced at him curiously. 'If you don't care what your mother thinks, why introduce me to her at all?'

His mouth tightened, his fingers flexing once more on the

steering wheel. 'She's family,' he said shortly, and Meghan knew it was time to drop the subject.

A few minutes later they entered a residential section of Milan, where the elegantly fronted town houses were as grand as small *palazzos*. On a large, sweeping square with a fenced green in the middle, Alessandro pulled his car to a stop.

'Here we are.' A dark-suited man had exited the house and approached the car before Alessandro had even killed the engine.

He opened Meghan's door and she clambered out, standing on the kerb while a brisk wind blew her hair into tangles.

The man opened Alessandro's door, and Alessandro tossed him the keys.

They exchanged some rapid Italian, and Meghan caught enough to understand that the man was taking the car round to the back.

'*Grazie*, Manuelo,' Alessandro said, and Manuelo gave a short bow. He asked something else in Italian, but the wind carried the words away. After hesitating for the briefest of seconds, Alessandro answered. Meghan heard her name being mentioned, and cast him a curious glance after Manuelo had left.

'What did you say about me?'

'You're staying here,' Alessandro explained briefly. 'I'll reside at my flat until our wedding.'

Alarm prickled along her spine. 'Why can't we stay together?'

Alessandro barely spared her a glance. 'It's not appropriate.'

Appropriate? Surely staying in separate rooms, chaperoned by Alessandro's own mother, was appropriate enough? Meghan wondered uneasily how Alessandro's attitude towards her might change now that she was becoming his wife and not just his lover.

And yet she knew he was doing it to protect her. To make her feel safe, secure, unashamed. Just as he'd promised. She smiled at him.

'Thank you.'

He shrugged in response. 'It is my duty.'

They entered the town house through a pair of impressive double doors covered with an intricate iron trellis.

The foyer was decorated in cool marble, with a crystal

chandelier suspended above a polished mahogany table with a large bowl of chrysanthemums on it.

Gabriella di Agnio entered from a short flight of steps that led to the rest of the house. She was a small, slender woman in her mid-sixties, dressed in a designer suit in cerise, her silver hair elegantly coiffed.

Meghan immediately felt gauche and underdressed, standing there, dazzled by wealth and glamour, dressed only in a jumper and jeans.

Gabriella's pale blue gaze swept over the pair of them before she inclined her head.

'Alessandro.'

Alessandro inclined his head back. 'Mamma.'

It was hardly a warm greeting, Meghan thought. Tension crackled in the air.

'I'm so glad you came. And your companion—Signorina Selby.' She smiled graciously at Meghan, and Meghan ducked her head back.

'Thank you.'

'Luncheon has been served in the dining room. Will you come?'

'Of course.' Alessandro put his hand on Meghan's back, propelling her forward with gentle pressure.

Gabriella watched this careless movement with narrowed eyes before smiling and leading the way upstairs.

Meghan imagined she could almost see the thread of hostility pulsating, taut and thin as a wire, between Alessandro and his mother. Why didn't they like each other? What had happened?

The dining room was a long, narrow room, with frescoes painted on the walls and ceiling. Meghan drew her breath at the beautiful and obviously old paintings. She'd seen similar work on the walls and ceilings of churches in Umbria and Florence.

The Di Agnios, she realised afresh, were rich. Powerful.

It was unfamiliar, and yet soon it would be hers. Hers.

The wealth…the safety.

The table was set with a fragrant dish of beef risotto. There was an opened bottle of red wine on the sideboard.

Alessandro and his mother sat at opposite ends of the long

polished table, and Meghan was forced to sit in the middle. She felt as if she were watching a tennis match.

'I didn't realise you were in Umbria,' Gabriella began, as she beckoned a servant forward to serve the risotto.

'Business,' Alessandro replied briefly.

'Are you back in Milan for long?'

Alessandro's mouth tightened imperceptibly. 'A few weeks. Maybe more.'

'Business is well?' Gabriella persisted, her voice eerily neutral.

'You should know—you check our stock prices every day.' Alessandro's mouth curled upwards in a mocking smile.

'I like to know what's going on. Now,' Gabriella replied with dignity.

'I know how much it pains you to see me at the helm,' he countered silkily, although his eyes glittered with—what? Meghan couldn't be sure. Rage?

Hurt?

'You almost wish I would make a mess of things, don't you, Mamma?' The word sounded crass. 'It would be easier for you, then, wouldn't it? You'd finally be justified.'

Gabriella dabbed at her lips with a linen napkin. When she raised her head to look at her son, her expression was stony.

'No, Alessandro. I don't want that.' She paused, a new bleakness in her eyes. 'I have never wanted to be justified.'

He shrugged—restless, unconvinced. 'I said almost.'

Meghan gazed down at the risotto on her plate, steaming and richly scented with saffron. Her mouth was so dry she didn't think she could manage a bite, delicious as it looked. She didn't want to look at either Alessandro or Gabriella, or to feel the bitter antagonism that vibrated between them.

She was relieved when the wine was poured, and she took a grateful sip of the rich, ruby liquid. It slid like velvet down her throat.

'What about you, Signorina Selby?' Gabriella turned her rather brittle smile on Meghan. 'Are you staying in Milan for long?'

'I…' Meghan looked helplessly at Alessandro. Obviously his mother was missing some salient details about their relationship.

'As a matter of fact, Mamma, Meghan will be staying as long as I am.' Alessandro smiled, but his eyes were cold and hard. 'We're getting married.'

The silence in the room was a physical thing, a separate presence, stifling, choking. Alessandro kept eating, and Meghan listened to the clink of his silverware while his mother simply stared, her face quite blank.

She recovered herself admirably, giving Meghan a forced but gracious smile. 'Then of course I must offer my felicitations. When is this wedding to be?'

'Next week.' Alessandro barely looked at her as he kept eating. Meghan stared down at her food. Colour scorched her face. She ate a forkful of risótto, and it turned to ash in her mouth.

'So very soon?'

He glanced up darkly. 'For the simple reason that I want to begin my new life with my bride, Mamma. No matter what conclusions you have jumped to about her or me.'

Good heavens, did Gabriella think she was pregnant? Meghan's cheeks burned hotter.

'I am very happy for both of you, then,' Gabriella said after a tiny pause.

There could be no mistaking that she was not pleased with this news. And what mother would be? Her son had brought home a stranger—one from another country, another *world*—and announced he was marrying her within a week.

Was this what Alessandro called appropriate?

'I'd appreciate it,' he said now, 'if you could take Meghan out to buy some suitable clothes. She has very little with her, and of course there is no one with better taste than you, Mamma.' Somehow he turned it into an insult. 'I will be quite busy for the next few days, managing some business from America.'

'I would be delighted.' Gabriella turned to Meghan with a smile that bordered on genuine. 'It will give me a chance to know my future daughter-in-law a bit better.'

Better than what? Meghan thought. A complete stranger? She pressed her napkin to her lips, suppressing the bubble of hysterical laughter that threatened to escape.

This was so, so crazy.

So wrong.

Yet when she'd been with Alessandro it had felt so *right*.

The man he'd been with her, alone in Umbria, was so different from this angry, haunted stranger.

Who was he?

Had she made the most enormous mistake of her life in agreeing to this?

And could she get out of it?

Somehow she thought that would prove difficult to do.

She glanced up, saw Alessandro take a sip of wine. He was gazing at his mother with a disappointed, almost sad look on his face, before the mask of masculine authority slipped back into place.

I'm not making a mistake.

Meghan clung to that hope, thin as it was.

Right now it felt as if it was all she had.

After lunch Alessandro excused himself to go to the office, announcing that he would be back for dinner. Gabriella showed Meghan to her room, tactfully suggesting she might appreciate a rest.

Meghan was grateful. Not only was she exhausted, but she couldn't endure an afternoon of strained conversation with Gabriella—and she had a feeling the older woman felt the same.

She drew the heavy brocade drapes, kicked off her shoes, and crawled under the soft duvet, closing her eyes against the oppressive environment of the house around her, the tensions unspoken, unrecognised, and yet so very evident.

Sleep came with blessed speed.

When she awoke the room was in shadow, late afternoon sunlight filtering through the crack in the curtains. She stretched, luxuriating in the warm, comfortable bed, knowing the memories and fears would rush back soon enough.

Then she realised someone was sitting on the edge of the bed, watching her.

It was Alessandro.

She gave a soft little gasp of surprise and tried to sit up. He stayed her with one hand on her leg, his touch burning even through the heavy material of the duvet.

'Don't. You looked so relaxed, so at peace. I've never seen you sleep before.'

His voice was soft, his face cloaked in shadow. Gently he stroked the length of her leg, and Meghan felt the stirrings of the desire that he so easily evoked in her.

'I was tired.'

'I know.' There was a smile in his voice, she knew, even though she couldn't see it. She heard it—heard the tenderness. 'It hasn't been easy for you. I'm sorry. My mother…'

'Why doesn't she like you?' Meghan asked, glad for the darkness that cloaked her question. 'And why don't you like her? You could have given me a little warning, Alessandro.' She didn't mean to sound reproachful, and she tensed for the anger, the withdrawal she was sure would come.

Instead he sighed with an aching weariness. 'You agreed to marry me, didn't you? Just me. Not my mother. Not anyone else.'

'Yes, but other people affect us. They matter.'

His hand moved up her leg to the joining of her thighs, fingers deftly, knowingly moving, stirring delicious feelings inside her. She found herself parting her legs, gasping as he teased her through the covers.

'Alessandro…'

'No one needs to matter,' he murmured, his voice a caress, a promise. 'No one needs to matter but us.'

He moved his hand treacherously upwards, creating flames of need everywhere he brushed his fingers. Across her navel, over her breasts, and then her face. He cupped her cheek, leaning forward so he was almost on top of her. She arched upwards, wanting the contact, the closeness. The touch.

'I look forward to mattering to you very much.'

He stretched out on top of her, and everywhere his body touched hers it burned. Ached.

Meghan moved as a matter of instinct, pressing against him, desiring more, wanting more.

Wanton.

'I think,' Alessandro whispered, 'it will take a long time. A lot of…experience.'

His hand left her face, slid under the duvet with practised ease to caress her breast, teasing her nipple to an aching peak through the soft fabric of her jumper.

Meghan moaned slightly, pushing herself against his hand. She saw Alessandro watching her, his eyes dark, intense, taking pleasure in her pleasure, in the response he so easily evoked in her. His own breathing was ragged, and she could feel the evidence of his desire.

'Alessandro…'

'I want you.' He moved his hands to cup her face once more. 'I want you so much.'

She reached up with her arms, running her fingers through the crisp softness of his hair, pulling his face down to hers.

'Meghan…' he groaned, then captured her mouth with his own. The kiss was deep, demanding, endless.

Needy.

Meghan revelled in the feel of him, the taste of him, in the knowledge that he wanted her as much as she wanted him.

He ended it first, pulling away with a ragged gasp.

'*Gattina*, I can't stand much more of this.'

There was a deep, restless ache of longing within her. A hunger demanding to be satisfied, a thirst to be quenched. Meghan closed her eyes, her own breathing uneven.

'Neither can I.'

'We will be married as soon as it can be arranged.'

Meghan pulled at him, wanting him closer. *Wanting* him. The pulsing ache in her needed to be eased. 'Alessandro…'

He covered her seeking lips with his fingers. 'We will wait till we are wed. Difficult as it is…and, *da tutti i san*, it is difficult for me.'

She gave a little groan. 'Who made that rule?'

Alessandro chuckled. 'I suppose that is up for debate. But I'm making it now. When we make love there will be no shame. No shadows.'

Meghan wanted to argue. The need, the desire was so strong.

She wanted to tell him there were no shadows. But she knew she would be lying.

She needed to tell him something else first.

'All right,' she said as she pushed up to a sitting position. 'I can wait. I have as much self-control as you do.'

'I look forward to shattering it one day soon,' Alessandro said softly.

He was so patient with her, Meghan realised. So tender. Even though he didn't love her. Perhaps it could be enough for them to build a life, a marriage upon. The thought gave her hope; it made her happy. 'You're a good man, Alessandro.'

He stilled, tensed, swinging around to look at her with a gaze that was dark and unyielding. Cold. 'Why do you say that?'

Meghan shrugged, discomfited by his sudden change of mood, his quiet, lethal tone. 'Because you are.'

He shook his head; Meghan thought she heard him laugh softly. She didn't like the sound.

'Dinner is in half an hour. My mother keeps a formal table. Will you be ready?'

A formal table? With a rush of nerves, Meghan realised she didn't have anything appropriate to wear. 'I'm afraid my haversack doesn't hold evening gowns,' she joked, but Alessandro just shrugged.

'There are some clothes in the cupboard in this room. I imagine something suitable can be found there. And tomorrow you will go with my mother to buy a new wardrobe, as I said.'

Meghan gave him a teasing little smile. 'And who do *these* clothes belong to?'

Alessandro watched her for a moment, his face expressionless, his tone bland. When he spoke, it was with cold decision. 'I imagine,' he replied, 'they belong to one of my mistresses. I will see you at dinner.'

He slipped from the bed and the room, leaving Meghan alone in the darkness with the shock and pain caused by a comment so cruelly, so casually delivered.

CHAPTER EIGHT

'I THINK we will find all that you need on the Via Montenapoleone,' Gabriella told Meghan the next day, as they took the di Agnio limousine into Milan's shopping district. 'The best shops are there— including the flagship Di Agnio boutique.'

Meghan nodded, barely taking in her future mother-in-law's words. She was hopelessly distracted by the remorseless echo of Alessandro's voice.

One of my mistresses.

After he'd left the room Meghan had opened the cupboard and found a range of clothes, from casual dresses and jeans to screamingly expensive evening gowns.

His mistresses' clothes.

Why had he said that?

Meghan had sighed as she'd taken in one designer gown after another, her hands roaming mindlessly over silk, satin and crêpe. Of course she'd known he'd had lovers. Mistresses. He was a virile, beautiful man. Of course he had. He'd hinted at it before.

But why mention it then, in the twilit intimacy of the darkened bedroom, her lips still burning from his kisses, her senses still scattered by his touch? The remark had been delivered with the cruel, cold accuracy of an arrow to the heart…and it had met its target.

He had, Meghan knew, been warning her.

Don't fall in love with me. The voice in her head was as loud as if he'd actually said it.

And hadn't he? He'd warned her before. She should have realised a single moment of tenderness, companionship, desire was simply that.

A moment in an otherwise barren marriage.

A marriage of convenience...for both of them. No matter how it felt, no matter how it seemed.

He wanted someone to give him an heir. A willing woman in his bed who wouldn't demand love. Someone to keep him from being alone. Lonely.

A woman who wouldn't *bother* him too much.

And she wanted power. Safety. Security. Release from the fear and shame.

That was why she'd agreed. *That* was the promise she would build her life upon.

Not flimsy dreams of love, of affection, but the man Alessandro had said he meant to be.

She'd finally picked one of the gowns—a simple design of black silk that had swirled about her calves and was the least revealing—and had gone downstairs.

Dinner had been stilted, strained. Gabriella had tried to make conversation, Meghan had helped her woodenly, and Alessandro had sat in flinty silence, preoccupied, refusing even to meet Meghan's gaze, indifferent to his mother's.

After dinner he'd excused himself, and when Meghan had woken in the morning he'd already gone to work. She wondered if she'd actually see him again before the wedding.

The wedding. She could leave, she reminded herself. Slip out while he was at the office and never come back.

Keep running.

The trouble was, she didn't want to.

She was damned by her own need.

Her own desire.

'Here we are.' Gabriella's voice was bright, her manner only a little stiff, as the car slowed to a stop on a long, glittering street lined with the most famous and expensive designer names in the world. Boutiques with a single garment hanging in the window and a lock on the door.

The next few hours were a blur of clothes and fitting rooms. Gabriella spoke rapid Italian with sleek saleswomen who examined Meghan's body and thrust clothes at her as if she were no more than a problem, a rather difficult problem, to be fixed.

Three hours and a dozen designer bags later, Gabriella glanced consideringly at Meghan and said, 'I know Alessandro has not mentioned it, but since you are to be married, perhaps we could do your hair? Your make-up? There is a salon on the next street that can take you now.'

Meghan nodded dumbly. She hadn't had a haircut in over six months.

'*Buon.*' Gabriella smiled. 'As sudden as this arrangement may be, every bride wants to look beautiful on her wedding day, yes? And what of your dress?'

'Dress?' Meghan repeated uncertainly. She was humbled by Gabriella's acceptance, by the woman's friendliness.

'Wedding dress,' Gabriella explained. 'There are few shops that can fit and alter a dress in so short a time.'

'It's going to be a very small wedding,' Meghan said hurriedly. 'I can wear something simple. One of the dresses you bought for me.'

'No, that will not do. You need a proper dress—a bride's dress.' Gabriella paused. 'You can wear mine.'

'What?' Meghan was stunned.

Gabriella laughed lightly. 'I know, it is old—but they call it vintage these days, yes? And it is a timeless classic, I assure you. I have a seamstress who can alter it in a matter of hours.'

'I can't—' Meghan began, and Gabriella fixed her with a pale, penetrating stare so similar to her son's.

'But why not? You are marrying my son, are you not? You are going to be my daughter-in-law. You need a dress. Of course, if you don't like it you must not wear it. We can find something else.'

'It's not that.' Meghan stared down at her hands. 'It's just…' She looked up, open, honest. She had to know. She would not start this life, begin in this family, with mistrust. 'Why don't you hate me?'

Gabriella looked taken aback. 'But why should I hate you?'

'I've known Alessandro for a very short while. I'm not from your…class.' She stumbled over the words, the explanation. 'I'm not even Italian. Perhaps you had someone in mind for him already…'

Gabriella shook her head. 'No, my dear. The only thing I have in mind for Alessandro now is his own happiness.'

'Yet…' Meghan swallowed. 'There's so much tension between you.'

Gabriella smiled, the movement strained. 'Alessandro is very angry with me.' She paused, weighing her words. 'I have not considered his happiness in the past as much as I should have. In all honesty, I have not considered…him. It was easier to forget. And then there was the—'

'Forget your own son?' The words came out before Meghan could stop herself, and she winced as pain shadowed Gabriella's features.

'Alessandro was not an easy child—nor, for that matter, is he an easy man. I realise now my own blame in who he became. It is why he is so angry.' She shrugged sadly. 'If you make him happy, then how can I complain?'

'I hope I will,' Meghan whispered.

'You will.' Gabriella shrugged off the serious talk. 'With your new hair and make-up, in my wedding dress… *Da tutti i san!* Who could resist you?'

Meghan found herself smiling back. '*Da tutti i san,*' she repeated. 'Alessandro says that. What does it mean?'

'By all the saints. His grandmother used to say it a lot. He was…very close to her.'

Meghan was intrigued by this glimpse into an Alessandro she didn't know, couldn't fathom. 'Did she die?'

'When he was nine. She lived in Umbria, at the villa.' Gabriella shot her a quick, speculative look. 'You know it?'

'Yes.' Meghan couldn't keep a tell-tale flush from warming her face. 'I thought it had belonged to Alessandro's father.'

'Yes, it was my husband's family home.'

'And then Alessandro's brother's?' Meghan pressed, seeking more information.

Gabriella's lips pressed together. 'Yes, it belonged to Roberto. Now it is Alessandro's, as perhaps it should have been all along. Enough talk. We must eat. Shopping is hard work. And tonight you can show Alessandro your purchases. He will be pleased, I hope.'

Meghan nodded. Her stomach had turned queasy, roiling with nerves and doubts. The last time she'd seen Alessandro he hadn't looked pleased at all, about anything.

About her.

Had he changed his mind?

With lurching fear, she realised she didn't want him to. How had she started to believe in this, in *them*, so quickly? So *much*?

Especially when she didn't even know what *them* meant—what they would be to each other. How a marriage would *work*.

That evening Meghan gazed at her reflection in amazement.

The clothes had been put away, she'd had a nap, and she'd awoken refreshed, ready.

And beautiful.

She touched her hair, now highlighted and styled in gentle waves to her shoulders. The hairdresser hadn't changed her look; he'd just made her better. More herself.

It had taken, Meghan acknowledged wryly, a lot of money to accomplish that.

The make-up she'd painstakingly applied emphasised her golden-green eyes, making her lashes thick and long, sweeping down to delicately tinted cheeks. Her lips were full and sensual without being pouty. She smiled, intrigued by her new self.

She glanced down at herself, dressed in one of the gowns purchased that morning. It was a pale amber, the colour of morning sunlight.

'It complements your eyes,' Gabriella had said in approval. 'Very nice.'

Looking at herself, Meghan had to agree. The dress was simple, pouring over her body like liquid sunshine without being too revealing, too obvious.

Hinting, not screaming.

Promising.

Taking a deep breath, Meghan turned away from her reflection, the image in the mirror having bolstered her confidence enough. It was time to go downstairs and meet Alessandro.

The central staircase of the town house twisted in a spiral down to the foyer, and as Meghan descended the marble steps she saw Alessandro at the bottom, dressed in a navy blue suit, his back to her. One hand was shoved in his trouser pocket, the other raked through his ebony hair.

Meghan paused on the step, silent and watching. Watching him. Was she imagining the vulnerability in his stance? She must be, for every lithe movement radiated power, strength, authority. Control.

Need.

The word came from nowhere; the thought was stunning in its force.

Surely Alessandro could never need anything?

Surely he could never need her?

Need was more than desire.

Need was love.

He turned, and his eyes blazed for a moment, sweeping over her, drinking her in.

Meghan felt heat everywhere his eyes roamed. Treacherous, wonderful heat. It weakened her, made her sway, and Alessandro saw and smiled.

He reached for the banister, gripped it hard, and Meghan realised with a ripple of shock that he was just as affected as she was.

She walked on trembling legs down the last few steps into the foyer.

'Hello, Alessandro.'

He reached for her fingers, gently pulling him to her. His lips brushed hers, and when he spoke it was a whisper against her mouth.

'Why don't you hate me?'

Meghan tensed, startled. 'Why would I hate you?'

He kissed her again, moved his lips to her temple. 'I didn't mean to hurt you, *gattina.*'

Yes, you did. Meghan smiled through the sudden sting of tears. 'It's all right.'

'No.' His voice was low and almost savage. He kissed her again, hard on the mouth, his fingers digging into her shoulders before he relaxed, his hands softening into a caress. 'No,' he said against her lips. 'But it will be.'

He stepped back, scorching her with one primal, possessive look. 'You look ravishing.'

He took her hand, linking their fingers as he led her into the dining room.

'So,' Gabriella began when they were seated, the food served and wine poured, 'you say this wedding is next week? Have you made preparations? Secured a church?'

Meghan glanced enquiringly at Alessandro, as curious to know the details as her future mother-in-law.

'We will be married on Friday, at the San Pietro church,' Alessandro informed them both. 'There will be a reception afterwards at the Principe di Savoia.' He glanced at Meghan. 'I would have left the arrangements to you, but you are a stranger to this city. I thought it would be easier to arrange it all myself. I hope that is agreeable to you?'

'Of course,' she murmured.

'The Principe di Savoia is Milan's most luxurious hotel,' Gabriella informed her. 'You will be well served there.' She turned to Alessandro, her thin eyebrows raised. 'And how many guests are you inviting to this celebration, may I ask? Have you taken care of the invitations as well?'

'It will be a small affair, as Meghan and I both want. Family only. A few friends.' He smiled, his voice becoming a drawl. 'You must invite who you like though, Mamma. I imagine you have plenty of friends who are eager to witness the spectacle…your prodigal son getting married.'

'Thank you.' Gabriella clearly chose to ignore the jibe. 'Chiara is coming?'

'I spoke to her on the telephone,' Alessandro confirmed. 'She can only come for the day. You know how busy she is.'

'How busy she chooses to be,' Gabriella agreed. 'And what of your family, Meghan?'

'I don't have anyone coming.' It came out as a wretched confession. Meghan lifted her chin. 'I've been travelling for a while now, and I've…lost touch with people from home.'

Gabriella maintained an eloquent silence at this news, and Meghan knew how odd it must sound. No friends, no family?

No one.

She took a bite of the antipasti—rigatoni in a delicate cream sauce. When would she tell her family? she wondered. When would she go back?

The thought was too depressing, and so she pushed it away. There was enough to deal with here. She had her own shadows, but so did Alessandro.

She wondered if she would ever find out what they were.

After dinner Gabriella excused herself, and Alessandro and Meghan were left alone in the elegant drawing room that faced the front of the house.

A tension thrummed between them, taut and expectant. Meghan realised they hadn't had much experience in being alone, living as a couple, doing normal, boring things.

The intensity remained. It wouldn't go away.

How long could they keep this up?

She moved around the room, seeking bland conversation, something innocuous, safe.

Like the villa, the drawing room was decorated in shades of cream and ivory, the muted colours punctuated by the vivid oil paintings on the wall.

Meghan inspected one while Alessandro poured them drinks.

'Is this by the same artist as the ones in the villa?' she asked. 'I don't know much about art, but it looks similar.'

'So it is,' Alessandro agreed, his voice neutral. She knew he was at his most dangerous when his face turned blank, his voice toneless, the mask dropping into place.

She needed to be careful. She needed to know.

He knocked back half of his *negroni* before handing Meghan her own glass.

'Who is the artist?' she asked, and Alessandro took another sip of his drink.

'My brother. You can see my parents were very fond of his work. They have his paintings in nearly every room of this house.'

Meghan studied him, his careless pose, and yet there was restless energy radiating from every taut line of his beautiful body. The mood had suddenly turned sour, savage, and she wasn't sure why. 'Are you jealous of him?' she asked uncertainly, and he raked her with a cool, contemptuous gaze.

'Jealous? He's dead. What is there to be jealous of?'

'I meant before that.' Meghan spoke cautiously, feeling each word as though in a darkened maze of memories, every turn leading to an unforeseen trap. A danger.

'Was I jealous of my brother?' Alessandro spoke musingly, his expression distant. 'Perhaps I was, a little. You've given me an amusing bit of therapy there.' His tone turned sardonic. 'I'd never considered that before.'

'Don't.' Meghan put her glass of *negroni* down, untasted. 'You sound like a little boy—mad at his mother, jealous of his brother.'

His eyes turned so dark she couldn't see his pupils. It was as if his muscles, his mood, were carved from ice. 'You know nothing about it.'

'No, I don't. So why don't you tell me?'

'I've told you all you need to know.'

'I want to know more,' she persisted, her voice breaking a little. 'Alessandro, I want to understand you.'

He laughed, a harsh sound, raking a hand through his hair before setting his glass down so hard it rattled. 'Trust me, Meghan,' he said savagely, 'you do *not* want to understand me.'

Meghan trembled inwardly at his words, but she stood her ground. 'Tell me why not, then.'

He glanced at her, eyes blazing, punishing. His smile was a cruel slash of colour on his face. She took an unsteady step backwards.

'Why do you think I chose you?' he asked, his voice a deadly purr. 'And not some Italian girl, like you said? Someone from my own class, culture? Because face it, Meghan...' he glanced at her with a searing contempt that made her feel tarted-up and dirty '…you're not.'

'I know I'm not,' she whispered, hurt despite her intention not to be, despite her realisation that he was trying to hurt her and she was letting him. This was perhaps hurting him as much as it was her.

Why did he do this to her? To himself?

Why?

'I chose you because you don't know my family, you don't know me, and it can stay that way. I don't *want* you to know me. I don't *want* you to understand me. I don't love you, and you don't love me, remember? So let's enjoy each other's company—and bodies—without any unnecessary complications. Is that understood?' His mouth turned upwards in a mocking smile.

Meghan stumbled back a step, sickened. 'What about the promises you made to me, Alessandro? What about *the man you mean to be*? Is this it? Because if so, I don't want any part of you.' The words rang out, echoing, condemning.

The smile died on his face, leaving it blank and empty. He stared at her for a moment, and Meghan opened her mouth to deny what she said, to apologise. She wanted him. She wanted *all* of him. She wanted to understand, to explain, to…

Help. Help him.

'It's too late for regrets,' he said tonelessly. 'For either of us. You will marry me, Meghan. You don't have any choice. And neither do I.'

'We both have choices,' Meghan protested, though her voice sounded feeble. 'This may have been a deal, Alessandro, but we can break it.' Not that she wanted to even now, God help her.

'We cannot!'

His hand slashed through the air, and, goaded, Meghan found herself replying, '*I* can.'

He came to her in two strides, his face lit with a primal ferocity as he grabbed her shoulders. 'You will not break it, Meghan. Swear to me!'

'Don't do this,' she whispered. Tears streaked down her face.

He released her. Then his hands slid down her arms, down her sides, and he fell to his knees, his head buried against her middle.

'I'm sorry,' he whispered, his voice jagged and broken. He drew in a shuddering breath and his arms wrapped around her waist, clinging to her as if she were his anchor. 'I never meant… What kind of man am I?' It came out as an anguished cry, a plea for mercy. '*What kind of man am I?*'

Meghan trembled with suppressed emotion, pain. The tears still streaked down her face as she buried her fingers in his hair. He lifted his head to gaze up at her. The bleak despair etched in harsh, unforgiving lines on Alessandro's face was nearly her undoing.

'The man you mean to be,' she whispered, and kissed him with all the tenderness she longed to give him. He knelt there, motionless, accepting her offering, before he pulled her down to him, turning the kiss into something deeper, something that hurt like a wound, deep inside.

His arms were around her, hard and desperate, the kiss plundering, plunging. Meghan kissed him back, desire fanning quickly, leaping into dangerous flames. She threw her head back to give him access to her throat, desire now pouring through her in a molten wave, burning her up. Their breathing was harsh, ragged.

He pulled her dress down, mindless of the delicate material. The sound of its tearing rent the air, and his voice came out in a sob as he buried his head between her breasts, touching her, suckling her, turning her to liquid fire even as the tears dried on her cheeks.

She pulled open his shirt, the buttons popping and scattering across the floor, let her hands touch and twist and tease, before wrapping her arms around the smooth, broad expanse of his back, pulling him closer.

She didn't know what was happening—why this moment of passion had sprung from pain and despair, sorrow and misery.

She only knew that she wanted to satisfy him—that she was his, she *would* be his.

It was what he needed.

And she needed it too; her body ached, demanding to be

quenched. She pulled him to her, her dress bunched around her waist, her thighs bare and splayed open.

Alessandro was poised above her, one hand on the waistband of his trousers, undoing his fly with urgent trembling fingers, when he suddenly stilled. Stopped.

The moment was endless. She looked up from the haze of her own need and desire and saw a terrible anguish on his face. He dropped his hand from his trousers, rolled off her onto his back on the floor, one arm covering his face.

'Alessandro…'

'Heaven help me,' he choked out. 'Look at us. Look at *me*.' He sounded disgusted, sickened.

'I'm sorry…' Meghan began hesitantly. She lay there, her dress in hopeless disarray, her body still open to him. Still wanting.

He didn't look at her as he shook his head. '*You* are sorry? *Gattina*, no. *No*.' It came out harshly. He dropped his arm from his face, sat up and raked a hand through his hair, his face still averted. 'Just go, Meghan,' he said in a low voice. 'Leave me. I'm no good to you now.'

Meghan sat up too, pulled her dress back on with trembling fingers. She wanted to touch him, wanted to put her arms around his hunched shoulders, stroke his bowed head. 'Yes, you are.'

He shook his head again, his hands fisted in his hair. '*Please*. Please leave me. For both our sakes.' His voice rose to a near roar. 'Go!'

Choking back the misery and confusion that threatened to rise up into an endless sob, Meghan went.

CHAPTER NINE

THE wedding was a blur.

Meghan understood the words, but the Italian washed over her in a soothing, melodious tide of language.

She wore the dress—Gabriella's timelessly elegant ivory gown—altered to fit her own more generous curves.

She saw the guests, a handful of discreet friends and business associates who watched the strange, sudden ceremony with carefully blank faces.

She had the bridesmaids—Alessandro's younger sister, Chiara, sleek and quiet, having flown in that morning from London. She was flying out immediately after the reception, and from the way she stood next to Meghan, her body tense and straining as the priest rambled on, Meghan guessed she couldn't get out of there fast enough.

Alessandro's best man, Stefano Lucrezi, was watchful and alert, his attention solely on the priest. Meghan had the sense that he was aware in some way of Chiara, though he never looked at her.

And Alessandro? He stood there, calm, urbane, implacable. In a few minutes—seconds, perhaps—he would be her husband.

He hadn't spoken one word to her since she'd entered the church, walked down the ancient stone aisle alone amidst a sea of frighteningly neutral faces.

This was her life now.

Now, *now* it was too late to back out.

And still she didn't want to.

Silly, naïve her.

After that shattered evening when they'd almost made love—passionate, desperate, on the floor—Alessandro had reverted to his old self: charming, urbane, amusing.

A fake.

Meghan saw it now—saw how the mask dropped into place, saw how he protected himself, kept anyone from guessing, knowing who he really was.

She still didn't.

And yet she was here, marrying him, because she wanted to know.

It wasn't just about the power any more.

It was about the need.

The priest stopped talking, and Meghan saw that the guests had all stood. Waiting.

She was married.

Alessandro took her cold hand in his, and together they walked out of the church into the pale sunshine of the early spring day.

Everyone else followed them out before either of them had exchanged a word. Stefano clapped Alessandro on the shoulder, and Meghan recognised the various phrases of congratulation, though she felt numb to the emotions.

Someone brought forward a beribboned box, gesturing excitedly for Meghan to open it.

She looked uncertainly from the box on the steps of the church to Alessandro, whose expression was inscrutable.

'They want you to open it,' he explained, with a slight smile, and Meghan moved forward. Was it a present? A custom? She wished Alessandro would explain, but he'd only folded his arms over his chest, his eyes glinting with cool amusement.

'You could help me a little,' she said under her breath, and Alessandro smiled.

'But I'm enjoying the view from here.'

Meghan gritted her teeth. Charming, aloof, distant. This was the man he chose to be now, and she would have to accept it.

She couldn't make him bare his true self. Wasn't sure she was ready for it. The glimpse she'd had so far had shot her to pieces.

She pulled on the ribbons and tentatively opened the lid of the box.

There was a loud cooing sound, the rushing of wings, and she stumbled back in surprise, her arms thrown over her face, as two doves soared into the sky amid many exclamations and cheers.

'An Italian tradition,' Alessandro informed her dryly as she lowered her arms and gazed upwards at the birds, now circling the church spire. 'To symbolise the happiness and unity of the married couple. My mother arranged it, no doubt. Reading things into this marriage that are not there.'

Meghan was struck to her soul, but she mustered enough spirit to reply in kind. 'What? You don't want happiness? Surely *that's* a reasonable expectation for both of us, Alessandro?'

'Is it?' There was no mistaking the sardonic doubt in his voice.

'Yes,' Meghan said firmly, daring him to believe, wanting to believe herself. 'It is.'

He gazed down at her, and a reluctant smile tugged at his mouth. 'As long as you realise what makes us happy.'

What made *him* happy. More warnings. Meghan was tired of it. 'Don't flatter yourself,' she hissed under her breath. 'I'm not in that much danger of falling in love with you!'

Alessandro's face relaxed and he gave a little chuckle. 'I'm glad to hear it. I like your claws, *gattina*. And perhaps we *shall* both be happy.'

He took her elbow, steering her through the crowd into the waiting limo that would take them to the reception.

'Who are all those people?' Meghan asked as she craned backwards to look at the milling crowd.

'Mostly business associates, friends of my mother's.' He shrugged in dismissal.

'What about your friends?'

He smiled, but his voice was hard. 'My friends were not invited.'

What on earth did that mean? Meghan leaned back against the seat and closed her eyes. 'But you have friends,' she said after a moment. 'Will I meet them?'

'No.'

End of discussion. Right now Meghan was too tired to press, too weary to hear his warnings, his rebukes.

'What a pair we are,' she said, trying to make her voice light. 'Friendless and alone.'

'That's why I married you, isn't it?' Alessandro returned silkily. 'Now we're not alone. Now we have each other.'

Somehow his lethal, mocking tone robbed the words of any comfort.

The reception was in a private room at the Principe di Savoia, one of Milan's most elegant hotels. Meghan sat down, ate the delicious food, drank the exquisite wine, and accepted the embraces and congratulations from a crowd that had become loosened and relaxed, ready to celebrate.

Alessandro sat in the middle of it all, dark and forebidding. When he greeted someone his voice was polished and smooth; he laughed at the jokes and participated in the customary dances, even La Tarantella, the circle dance that Meghan stumbled through, uncertain of the steps, distant from the jollity.

Yet there was no mistaking his dark preoccupation. Almost, Meghan thought sadly, as if he wanted to be somewhere else.

Be someone else.

Her stomach churned. Her heart twisted. Doubt washed over her, yet she couldn't regret. She'd made this decision. She'd wanted to be here.

Only she hadn't realised just how very hard it would be. How very hard *Alessandro* would be, his mouth a grim line, his eyes flinty, every taut line of his body making him guarded, unapproachable.

Unlovable.

How many secrets, dark and treacherous, churned and seethed in the space between them, creating an impossible chasm?

And they weren't even her secrets.

They were his.

When she was alone for a moment, scraping her sanity together as she stood by a pillar at the side of the dance floor, Stefano Lucrezi approached her.

'Congratulations, Signora di Agnio.' His voice was smooth and pleasant, yet the title jolted her.

'Thank you, Signor Lucrezi.'

'Please, call me Stefano. So, this was quite the love match?' He raised his eyebrows, smiling at her. 'I've never known Alessandro to move so quickly with a woman before.'

'Is that so?' Meghan's own smile turned brittle. 'He has taken care to warn me that he has moved quite quickly with plenty of women in the past.'

Stefano's gaze did not falter. 'Ah, so you know of his reputation?'

His reputation? It sounded bad. Still, if the secret that rode Alessandro, drove him to despair, was simply having had too many affairs, Meghan thought she could accept it. She didn't like it, but if it was the reality she would learn to deal with it.

'No one's told me much of anything,' she said frankly. She looked at Stefano. He seemed friendly, open, and she wanted answers. 'Do you know Alessandro well?'

'As well as anybody does. He keeps to himself.'

'Sometimes,' Meghan said quietly, her voice an ache, 'I think I know him quite well. And at other times not at all.'

'He is, perhaps, two different people,' Stefano said after a moment. 'The man he was, and the man he is now.'

And the man he meant to be. 'What do you mean, exactly? What happened to change him?'

Stefano shook his head. 'It is not for me to say.' He patted her hand gently. 'Perhaps he will tell you, *signora*, in time.'

Sketching a slight bow, Stefano left her.

Meghan sagged against the pillar behind her. She'd been given clues to this impossible, unfathomable man, but she didn't understand what they meant.

Didn't know if she could keep digging for answers.

Wasn't sure she wanted to find out.

Across the room Alessandro watched his bride with a cold detachment he was far from feeling. Encasing himself in ice was the only way to get through this event, when every pair of eyes watched him speculatively, hungrily, waiting for disaster, shame.

His own.

They all wanted him to fail—expected it. He'd lived with that for two years, and it should mean nothing to him now.

It *did* mean nothing to him—except for the one person in the room who didn't understand.

The one person he couldn't bear to see him fail.

And yet he would fail. Not with business, because he was good at that. He'd surprised everyone, especially himself, when he'd taken the reins of his father's company and found that he held them with natural ease.

He would fail *her*. He already had, in so many ways, and he saw it in the stark confusion in her eyes—the way she turned towards and away from him at the same time, because she didn't know what he would do, who he was.

What he was.

'I just spoke to your bride.' Stefano stood by Alessandro's chair, smiling faintly. 'She seems quite fond of you, my friend.'

'She'll learn better.'

'Do you love her?'

Alessandro laughed shortly. 'No. Of course not.'

Stefano nodded musingly, although his voice sounded regretful. 'It's easier that way, I suppose.'

Alessandro turned to him, raised one eyebrow in mocking incredulity. 'You're not going to tell me you believe in true love?'

'Of course not.' Stefano smiled tightly. 'You know as well as I do that such a thing is a fairytale. We're wise men, Alessandro.'

'Yes,' he replied flatly, his eyes fastened on Meghan's slight form. 'We are.'

It was time to end this torture. He could not take any more speculation, whispered gossip. He wanted to be alone. He wanted to be with Meghan.

It was time to claim his bride.

She felt someone's gaze on her, and before she turned, before she saw who it was, she knew.

The heat and the desire turned her limbs weak, her mind blank and yet flooded with feeling.

Alessandro.

Meghan turned, saw him watching her, a possessive smile quirking his lips.

He moved towards her, lithe and loose-limbed, an elegant stalking that she surrendered to completely.

'It is time to go.'

'Already?'

'The bride and groom must leave first. It is tradition.' His arm snaked around her waist and he pulled her to his side. 'And I can wait no longer. You look beautiful in that dress, *cara*.'

'It's your mother's. She was very generous to offer it.'

'Yes, I can see how she wants to make amends.' He brushed her hair with his lips. 'But I do not want to talk of her. There is a suite upstairs, waiting for us.'

Meghan's stomach plunged with nerves. She wanted this, she reminded herself. She wanted this so very much.

It didn't stop her from being scared.

'All right. Do we say goodbye?'

'Not unless you want lots of bawdy jokes and knowing looks.'

Meghan shuddered. 'I couldn't stand that.'

'Then we slip out now, quietly, when no one is looking.'

'What will people think?'

'That we can't wait to be alone with each other. And it's true…isn't it?'

She nodded shakily. 'Yes, it's true.'

Even if I'm terrified.

They were silent as they slipped from the reception, silent as they rode in the elevator to the top floor. Silent as Alessandro swiped the electronic key card and ushered her into a sumptuous suite of rooms.

Silent—yet the tension, the expectation, the desire, thrummed to life between them, more potent than any words or looks. It was a physical presence, a separate entity, and it filled the space with silent, urgent demand.

Meghan glanced around at the elegant chairs and sofas, the double doors that led into the bedroom. Her mind was blank and buzzing. 'This is very nice.'

'Do you want a bath? I've had your clothes brought from the town house.'

Meghan nodded numbly. 'Yes, fine.'

He walked over to her, skimmed his hands lightly over her bare shoulders. 'Don't be afraid, Meghan. There are no shadows here.'

But there were, she realised. There always would be. Because he didn't know. Didn't understand.

She couldn't make him tell her his secrets, but she could at least tell him her own. Banish her own shadows.

'I think,' she said jerkily, 'I'll have that bath.'

'*Buon*. I'll be waiting.'

Meghan sifted through her suitcase, found her toiletry bag, full of the new cosmetics, tubes and sprays and gels Gabriella had picked out for her, and the nightgown also selected by her mother-in-law—a sheath of ivory silk, held up with two tiny straps and scalloped with lace. She bunched the garment in her fist and, avoiding Alessandro's gaze, retreated into the bathroom.

The room was larger than her bedroom back at the hostel, a lifetime ago. Meghan turned the taps, added luxurious scented bath foam, carefully stripped off her wedding gown and slipped it on a hanger.

She stayed in the bath for half an hour, searching for her courage, clinging to what little she found.

Finally, reluctantly, her pulse thrumming—not just from the heat of the bath water—she rose from the tub and dried herself off, slipping on the bridal nightgown.

There was a thick terrycloth robe hanging on the door, provided by the hotel. Meghan slipped that on too.

Alessandro was stretched out on the bed, relaxed, his jacket and tie off, the top two buttons of his shirt undone. Just the sight of that little bit of clean, tanned skin caused Meghan's pulse to skitter higher.

He sat up when he saw her, taking in her bulky bathrobe with an ironic knowing look.

'You won't be needing that, will you?'

'No, but I want to talk to you first.'

A guarded expression came into his eyes, but he shrugged and patted the bed next to him. 'Of course. What about?'

'Me.' Meghan swallowed nervously and sat down. Her fingers fiddled with the sash of the robe. She couldn't look at him. 'Alessandro, I haven't told you everything about my past. About Stephen. I was too ashamed.'

'You want to tell me now?' His voice was carefully neutral.

'Yes. Because I don't want there to be secrets between us. My secrets.' Meghan forced herself to look up, meet his eyes. 'My shadows. And I want you to understand why I am...the way I am.'

He was quiet for a moment, his face blank. A mask. 'All right.'

Meghan took a deep, shuddering breath. This was so hard. Yet she knew she needed to do this.

Confession. Absolution.

'There was more to it than him just being married.'

Alessandro waited, silent. Meghan forced herself to continue. 'Stephen had always been handsome, charming. I knew he was a little racy, a little wild. I accepted it as part of him, and I loved him anyway. Or so I told myself. It's amazing the things you can convince yourself of when you're blind. In love.'

'Or naïve,' Alessandro added quietly.

Meghan nodded. 'I was all three. I accepted the sneaking around. I thought it was because he was a prominent business-man—a lawyer—and he didn't want to publicise his romantic re-lationships. I never thought that he thought...that he would...' She trailed off, staring down at her fingers still fiddling with the sash, her vision blurring.

'What did he think?' Alessandro asked, his voice soft, and yet with an underlying hardness that Meghan knew was not directed at her. 'What did he *do*?'

'The thing is,' she continued, her voice falsely bright, deter-mined, 'I should have known. I'm a modern, educated woman. Women like me don't get into situations where...'

Alessandro covered her hand with his own, stilling her nervous fidgeting. 'Where what?'

She squeezed his fingers, clutched them like a lifeline. 'Where you're controlled,' she explained quietly. 'First it was just how I was with him. I wanted to please him, to make him happy. He liked…certain things. Then it was what I wore, who I saw, what I said. He was jealous—horribly jealous, coldly jealous—and I thought it was love.'

Alessandro was silent for a moment, taking this in. 'He *did* abuse you,' he finally said flatly, still holding, stroking her fingers.

Meghan shook her head, denying the truth she'd suppressed for so long…the truth about Stephen, the truth about herself. 'But I *let* him. I should have known better. Everyone wondered what was happening to me—why I was so different, so distant. He didn't like my friends, my family, didn't like my life. I stopped going out… I lost my job because of it.' She closed her eyes briefly, recalling the pain, the shame. The obsession. The delusion. 'I told you Stanton Springs is a small town. Everybody watches out for everybody else. People *care.* They cared about me, and I just drove them all away. All that mattered to me was Stephen. I didn't know sometimes whether it was because of love or fear, but I couldn't leave him. I *couldn't.* How could I have been so blind? So *stupid*?'

'Our hearts are blind,' Alessandro said after a long moment. 'You thought he loved you.'

'If I'd had any self-respect—' Her voice caught jaggedly on a sob, then she choked it back. 'I would've walked out before it came to…before it brought me so low.'

Alessandro's eyes were gentle, but knowing. So knowing. 'What did he do to you?'

Meghan shook her head. She couldn't look at him. Didn't want to see disgust in his eyes, the disgust she'd felt herself, *at* herself. 'Nothing more than what he'd been doing before. Controlling me, humiliating me. He liked to see me under his thumb, catering to his whims, accepting his insults. Brought low. It gave him pleasure. I see that now, even though at the time I thought that was what you did when you loved someone. You just took it. You thought they'd stop. Change. I thought it was because I wasn't good enough, perfect enough. And then one night I'd had enough. I was so dispirited, so broken. I felt like I was dying inside—like all the good parts of me were gone. Used up. And I told him I'd had enough.'

'Did he let you go?' Alessandro asked quietly. Knowingly.

Meghan's hands clenched on the sash once more as memories assaulted her, battered her brain and heart. 'No. I should've realised he wouldn't. I told him I was sorry, that I loved him, and then…' She looked up now, met his gaze, faced the truth. 'He hit me. Across the face. I was so stunned I just lay there. I couldn't believe it. I was being *hit* by a man. The man I loved.'

'If I could get my hands on him…' Alessandro whispered savagely under his breath.

'He kept hitting me. I just took it. I was so surprised, so amazed it was happening. That I'd let it happen. It was my fault.'

'Meghan, it wasn't—'

She continued, determined to finish it to the end. 'He told me he was married then—said I must've known. He laughed about it. He said if I wondered why he treated me like a whore it was because I *was* one, and everyone knew it.' She closed her eyes briefly, shaking her head against the onslaught of memory. 'Of course, I knew he was lying. At least, my mind knew. My heart didn't. My heart believed every word he said.' She whispered the last, the confession echoing through her soul. She'd *believed*.

'What happened then?' Alessandro asked quietly, after a long moment when the only sound in the still room had been their breathing, ragged and uneven.

'I ran. He tried to grab me. I don't know what he would have done if— But I got away. And I kept on running. I ran right out of that town, that life, and I can't go back.'

'There are people there who would support you,' Alessandro said in a low voice. 'They would understand, Meghan.'

'But I'm so *ashamed*,' she confessed in a wretched whisper. 'It's my fault. I should have known. I should have known what kind of man he was. I should have stopped it.' Her voice broke, and Alessandro pulled her towards him, wrapped her in an embrace that was both tender and savage.

'No. How could you know? How could you expect…?'

He was silent, his arms around her, his chin resting on her head. Meghan tried to control her shuddering breaths, her pounding pulse.

'Did you press charges?' Alessandro asked after a long, ragged moment.

'No.' She was horrified at the thought. 'The last thing I wanted was people knowing what had happened, what I'd done. I told you—I ran. I didn't even explain where I was going. I sent a *postcard*. I know everyone is confused, hurt, even, but I couldn't live in that town knowing he was there. He wouldn't let me. And I couldn't bear people knowing.' She looked up at him, her eyes wide. 'I was afraid they would condemn me if they knew. I couldn't bear the shame.'

He stroked her face—light, feathering movements. 'No,' he said quietly, 'I don't suppose anyone could.'

He continued stroking her hair, her shoulders. Meghan never wanted him to let her go. She never wanted to feel alone, ashamed again.

'And for this you blame yourself?' he finally asked. 'You told me you thought you might have known deep down that he was married. I forced you to that confession.' Regret laced his words and roughened his tone. 'But this? Meghan, you could *never* blame yourself for this. That man—that Stephen—he was a monster. This was not your fault. None of it. You are not responsible for another's actions.'

'It's hard,' Meghan said after a moment, her voice no more than a thread of sound, 'not to blame yourself when someone else does. Someone you thought you loved. I stopped believing in myself, in who I *was*. I'm not sure if I even know any more.'

Alessandro was silent. Meghan heard their breathing, the ticking of a clock, the muted roar of traffic from Milan's busy streets below.

'Yes,' he agreed finally, softly. 'It is hard. Lord knows, it is very hard. But I am the man with you now, Meghan, *gattina*. I am the man who married you, and I believe in you.' He tilted her face up to meet his, wiped the traces of her tears with his thumbs. 'I *know* who you are, and I believe you.'

Meghan closed her eyes, felt the old shame slipping away. He knew. He knew, and he believed. 'Thank you,' she whispered. 'That's why I wanted to tell you.'

'I'm glad you did.' He cupped her face, slid his hand through the heavy mass of hair at the nape of her neck. 'Your trust in me is precious.' His voice was stilted, as if he was testing out new words, new emotions. 'I am humbled by it.'

Tears sparkled in her eyes. *Trust me.* She wanted to say it, to plead, but she knew now was not the time. She'd been ready to share, to confess.

Alessandro wasn't. Yet.

He gazed at her gently. 'And now? Are there shadows?'

Meghan smiled tremulously, glanced around the darkened room. 'No. There are no shadows for me.'

'Good.' He kissed her softly, the gesture a plea, a prayer. Not a demand. He would demand nothing of her tonight, Meghan knew.

Nothing that she didn't want.

She kissed him back, her hands sliding up the silkiness of his shirt, bunching the cloth between her restless seeking fingers.

He broke the kiss and glanced down at her with a faint frown between his brows. 'You are certain?'

'I am.' She felt drained, yet relieved. Empty, yet waiting to be filled.

'Good.' He kissed her again, this time his mouth sure and seeking, soft and warm.

Meghan felt him untie the bathrobe, felt it slip from her shoulders. She heard his indrawn breath as his gaze roamed over her, taking in the simplicity of the nightgown.

'You are so, so beautiful. *Bella.*' He kissed her shoulders, one first, then the other, and slipped the straps down. The material slid to her waist in a puddle of silk.

Meghan closed her eyes. She'd expected to feel exposed. Ashamed.

She felt neither.

She felt Alessandro's gaze on her—warm, admiring, gentle—and she smiled. He cupped her breasts in his hands, chuckling softly.

'As golden as the rest of you. You are like a sunbeam.'

She gave a little laugh, raised her eyes to meet his own heated gaze. 'I want to see you.' Fumbling just a little bit, she unbuttoned his shirt. He shrugged it off impatiently and she ran a hand down his chest, the smooth expanse of skin, sighing in satisfaction. 'I've wanted to do this.'

'I've wanted you to.' Alessandro's voice trembled as he laid her on the bed, stretching out beside her. 'This is how I've wanted it between us. Always.'

She nodded speechlessly, the feelings he was drawing from her filling her, spilling up to overflowing. She felt blessed.

He ran his hand over her breasts, across her navel, skimming over her hidden femininity.

Meghan moaned, arched helplessly. She wanted his touch. She craved it.

She lost herself to the exquisite feel of his hands on her, roaming, seeking, wanting. She was helpless, splayed beneath him, lost in sensation. Touch, taste, feel.

'Meghan, look at me.' There was amusement as well as tenderness in Alessandro's voice. 'Make love to me with your mind, not just your body. See the memory we're making together. See how I want you.'

Meghan opened her eyes, saw him braced on his forearms above her, the need and desire open in his face, his eyes, his languorous smile.

His hand moved down, deeper, slipping inside her with a gentle, knowing touch, to the very core of her womanhood, her self, stroking her to helpless flames.

She gasped, her eyes widening, fastened on his, as he smiled, his own eyes darkened with desire.

'Touch me.'

She touched his chest, let her hand slide down, her lips curving in an ancient, womanly smile of seductive power as she heard him gasp.

'Touch me…' His voice was ragged as he rolled on his back, taking her with him, giving her the power.

She straddled him, revelling in the feel of him underneath her, his hard thighs beneath hers, open, vulnerable to her, wanting her touch, her kiss, his entire body a supplication, a prayer.

She watched as his breathing hitched, his eyes glazed with

desire. He never stopped looking at her, even as he clasped her hips and she lowered herself onto him.

She gasped in shocked delight as she felt him fill her, felt the satisfaction deep in her core even as the hunger grew, wilder and deeper, needing to be met.

'You feel so good,' he said raggedly, 'so right.'

It did feel right, Meghan thought dizzily as she moved, rocking, adjusting to this new sensation, this wondrous flooding of feeling. Pleasure. Emotion. Joy. She threw her head back as they began to move in a beautiful dance, minds and bodies as one.

One.

One flesh.

She couldn't think any more, could only feel, her hands bunching on his arms, her thighs pressed against him as he reached up to cup her breasts in his hands, possess her in every way possible.

'Golden...' he whispered, chuckling softly, and Meghan gasped as he moved, clasping her to him, her legs wrapping around him so they were joined, fused, from shoulder to thigh. She buried her head in his neck, overwhelmed. Overcome.

'Look at me.'

I want you to see me when I make love to you. I want you to look in my eyes and see how I want you.

She saw it now as his eyes blazed into hers, filled with a desire that was elemental, consuming them both in its wondrous flames.

He never stopped looking at her, possessing with his eyes as well as his body, as the pressure and pleasure built to a glorious crescendo.

She cried out, and he captured her mouth with his own as she shattered, just as he had predicted she would, into a thousand sense-scattering pieces.

And then he put her back together again, cradling her as they lay there, still, sated, their breathing ragged.

I love you.

It came unbidden, helpless. Hopeless. Meghan closed her eyes, her cheek pressed against his chest, the tang of his sweat still on her lips.

I love you.
Why? When? How?

She didn't know when it had happened. Perhaps when she had first looked into his eyes at the trattoria, and her soul had recognised someone who knew her. Knew her completely and understood. Believed.

Perhaps it had happened later, when he'd opened her heart and mind to the possibility of trust, of desire without shame, need without fear.

Perhaps it had happened just now, when he'd undone her—known her—completely.

She just knew it was true.

She loved him—loved his tenderness, his teasing smile, his ability to give himself so completely. Loved him despite the darkness, the despair that he hid, the secrets she knew he kept, the pain she knew he would cause her.

She loved him.

And it was the last thing Alessandro wanted.

Alessandro listened as Meghan's breathing slowed, her breath feathering his chest. She was asleep.

He relaxed his arm around her, shifting to get more comfortable.

Except nothing could make him comfortable. Nothing could ease the guilt that ate at him, worse than any disease.

She doesn't know what kind of man I am.

He'd never realised how much she'd been through. Endured. His hand curled into a fist as he thought of what Meghan had been through, of the man who had abused her precious trust, her beautiful body.

He looked forward to going back to that hypocritical little town and wiping that man's face in the dirt.

Yet what help was that? *He* was the hypocrite; he was surely only going to cause her more suffering. He wouldn't be able to help it.

When she discovered his past...

When she learned who he really was...

What he was capable of. What he had done.

Then she would hate him. Affection would turn to disgust, love to hatred.

For he knew she would fall in love with him some time. It was in her nature, warm and generous.

No, he didn't want her to love him. Couldn't let it happen. He knew he wouldn't be able to bear it when it stopped.

And it would stop. Because he couldn't change. He couldn't be that man.

He couldn't be saved.

If only it were as simple as it had been for Meghan. Banishing the shadows and accepting forgiveness, love.

There was no such easy answer for him. People loved until you disappointed them. He'd seen it, lived it before. The moment you showed you were weak, needy, in pain or trouble, they left.

They fobbed you off on someone else. They turned away. They pretended they didn't know you.

And who could blame them?

He couldn't stand for that to happen to Meghan. Better for her not to love him at all.

The only way to keep her from falling in love with him, Alessandro knew, was to show her glimpses of the man he truly was.

Not enough to make her leave, but enough to make her wary.

He only prayed that he wouldn't hurt her too much…and that she would stay. It would be a fine line.

Because he didn't know what he would do if she left.

His arm tightened around her again instinctively, and she stirred in her sleep.

Glimpses, he reminded himself, his lips twisting in a savage smile. Glimpses would be enough.

CHAPTER TEN

MEGHAN awoke to an empty bed. For a moment she felt the familiar lurch of fear, then she forced herself to shrug it off.

There were no more shadows. For her.

Alessandro came into the room, showered, dressed, and bearing a tray with coffee and rolls.

'I thought you might be hungry.'

'Starving.'

His smile was knowing, seductive, and Meghan found herself grinning. She bit lustily into a roll as Alessandro took a cup of coffee and stretched out beside her.

'I thought today we could look for a place to live.'

'What about your flat?'

'It is a small place, sterile—a bachelor's pad, as they say. You would hate it.'

'I wouldn't,' Meghan protested. 'We could buy some flowers, some pictures—'

'No, no.' He was firm in his dismissal. 'It needs much more than that. It is simply not suitable. We can look for a place together—a home to start our new lives in?'

'If that's what you want,' Meghan said, a bit unsteadily. It sounded idyllic. Perfect. And far too good to be true. Like a dream they were weaving, something set apart. Unreal.

'That's what I want,' Alessandro replied. 'I need to make a few phone calls. I'll leave you to get dressed.'

He left the bedroom and Meghan leaned back against the

pillows, her mind buzzing happily with new thoughts, new dreams.

Half an hour later they were in Alessandro's car, cruising the streets of Milan.

Meghan gazed in wonder at the ancient buildings coupled with the modern glamour. This was Alessandro's city, she thought, as he navigated the traffic with expert and uncomplicated ease.

He belonged here, among the rich and powerful. And now she was part of that too. Yet somehow the prospect of power had lost its allure.

Wealth, security—even safety—they all seemed useless without love.

Meghan's mouth twisted grimly. Too bad, she thought. That was how it was. For now.

'Do you have a destination in mind?' she asked, and Alessandro gave her a fleeting smile.

'Wait and see…'

He turned the car into a narrow street which opened onto a square, not as impressive as at his mother's residence, but filled with sunlight.

Children played on the green, and the town houses that fronted it looked well cared for. Loved.

'This looks nice,' Meghan offered cautiously, for it wasn't the sort of place she'd imagined Alessandro in. It looked like a place for families—a place where happiness and joy were shared, simple pleasures enjoyed.

No glamour.

No power.

'Yes, it does,' he agreed. 'The agent gave me the key this morning.'

He led her up to one of the houses—a narrow stone building, with bright shutters and begonias spilling from the wrought-iron balconies.

Alessandro unlocked the door and ushered her inside.

Meghan walked slowly through the rooms. They were generously proportioned without being ostentatious, the wide windows thrown open to the spring sunshine.

She stood in the middle of the gleaming kitchen, the large pine table in its centre testifying to the fact that this was a family's house.

'It's semi-furnished,' Alessandro told her, reading the details from a brochure. 'We can pick up more bits and pieces as you like. Four bedrooms upstairs, another on the third floor if we want live-in help. The kitchen, lounge, and dining room on this floor. There is a small garden at the back, and of course the square out in front.' He looked up at her, eyes glinting. 'Do you like it?'

'It's perfect,' Meghan said simply. 'Perfect.'

He strode towards her, snatched her up and kissed her soundly. Meghan laughed in surprise.

'We'll have our children here. I'll teach our sons to play football in the square. It will be so good for us.'

His voice rang with certainty, and yet Meghan heard the desperation underneath, the ragged edges.

They were both trying so hard to believe. To make it real.

Yet it still smacked of a fairytale, a story that had to end— and perhaps not with a happily-ever-after.

They moved in the very next day. Alessandro had linens and towels brought from one of Milan's exclusive stores, and Meghan had fun shopping for food at the local *negozio*.

Alessandro came in from work as she made dinner, his gaze sweeping over the simple scene—from the food on the table to Meghan at the stove, a dishtowel tied around her waist.

'We forgot to buy an apron,' she said with a little smile, and he pulled her into a long, breathless kiss.

'I'd just want to take it off you anyway.' His hands roamed over her, leaving flames of need in their wake.

'Alessandro, the dinner…' Her protestation was so weak as to be laughable.

'We haven't christened this house,' Alessandro murmured against her mouth. 'I'd like to try every room—but we'll start with the bedroom. I like a soft bed…'

He pulled her upstairs, closing the bedroom door with a soft click, and laid her gently on the bed. Meghan lay there, happy, gazing up at him.

The look in his eyes—as if he were examining a priceless treasure—made her mouth dry. She held out her arms.

'Come to me.'

Pain slashed across his features so briefly she almost didn't notice it, but he shrugged off his clothes and fell upon her, and the moment of uncertainty was lost in passion, lost to the exquisite feeling of being touched, treasured.

'We've been invited to a party tomorrow,' Alessandro told her later, as they ate the reheated pasta, his voice suddenly turning alarmingly neutral. 'It's bound to happen as people hear about our wedding. They want to meet you.'

'A party could be fun,' Meghan said. She glanced at him uncertainly. 'You sound like you don't want me to meet them.'

'But of course not. I want to keep you all to myself. Any man would.'

'We can't hide for ever,' Meghan said teasingly, and knew immediately it had been the wrong thing to say.

A muscle bunched in his jaw and he set his wine glass down carefully. 'No,' he agreed flatly. 'We can't.'

What are you hiding? Meghan wanted to ask. Demand. *What secrets are you keeping?*

But of course she would demand nothing. Because Alessandro didn't want a wife who made demands.

A wife who loved him.

Too bad that was exactly what he had.

The next evening Meghan got dressed for the cocktail party with a mixture of anticipation and foreboding.

No matter what she'd said, she wanted to hide here with Alessandro for ever. Playing house and forgetting the world outside, the people who waited to meet them, to judge them.

Judge him.

'I have something for you.' Alessandro came in the bedroom, his black tuxedo setting off his ebony hair and navy eyes with stunning simplicity. He held a black velvet box in his hand.

Meghan turned, and he took in her evening gown—the amber silk she'd worn the other night, its tear discreetly mended—with an appreciative breath.

'My sunbeam,' he said softly. He handed her the box. 'This will match your gown and make your eyes sparkle.'

Intrigued, Meghan opened it. Nestled on the velvet was a necklace made up of pure topaz, the elegantly cut gems rimmed in gold, each piece daringly designed as if to fit a puzzle, sharp and brilliant.

'Alessandro, it's…amazing. Truly beautiful. Is it a Di Agnio piece?'

'As a matter of fact, yes. When I saw it I thought of you. May I?' She nodded, and he lifted the necklace from the box, slipping it around her throat.

It lay heavily against her collar-bone, each piece flat, shining. She touched it reverently. She'd never worn something so exquisite, so expensive.

Alessandro's appreciative smile hardened briefly. 'Now we must go. The party—and people—await.'

The cocktail party was in one of Milan's high-rises—a glittering needle of light that pierced the evening sky.

Meghan's nerves jangled as she thought of the people circulating above them, waiting for their arrival.

'We don't need to stay long,' Alessandro said, and she didn't know if he was reassuring her or himself. 'We're newlyweds, after all. People will understand.'

She nodded mutely, and a valet came to park the car.

Upstairs, guests mingled in a sumptuous penthouse apartment, the room filled with the murmur of voices and the clink of crystal.

Meghan searched the crowd for a familiar face and found none. She felt Alessandro tense beside her, though his urbane smile remained unchanged.

His whole body radiated tension. She wanted to reach out, to hold his hand, to tell him he could do this, *they* could do this, because she was at his side.

The idea was laughable. He would be furious that she saw his weakness, humiliated by her display. And she was too scared to do it anyway.

'Alessandro…and your lovely bride!' A man in his late forties, trim, with grey hair slicked back from a high forehead, came forward with a hard, bright smile. 'Who would ever have thought a man such as you would get married? It must be true love, eh?'

Alessandro inclined his head in cool acknowledgement. A muscle bunched in his jaw.

The man turned his crocodile smile on Meghan. She forced herself not to recoil from the way his gaze swept up and down her length. 'What is the trick, *bellissima*? To capture a man with such a—notorious—reputation with women?'

'I don't have any tricks,' Meghan replied with dignity. 'Perhaps that's why I have been successful where so many have not.'

'Ah, such a fair rose.' His smile verged on a sneer. 'Alessandro and I go way back, you know. We've shared many…experiences.' His voice caressed the last word with obvious lascivious intent.

'Experiences best forgotten,' Alessandro interjected lightly, although his eyes were like flint.

'I remember when you could have a woman on each arm and one in your lap, and be finished with all of them by midnight,' the man reminisced slyly. 'Good times, eh, Alessandro?'

'Things have changed.'

He raised one mocking eyebrow. 'Have they?'

Alessandro bunched his fist, flattened it. 'There are other people for us to greet, Bernardo.'

He turned his back on the man without another word.

'One of your friends?' Meghan asked in a low voice. She could feel the revulsion on her face, crawling along her skin, and she knew Alessandro could see it too.

He shrugged in reply. 'I told you—you don't know me.'

'I think I do know you,' Meghan replied. 'Even if I don't know who you were.'

He glanced at her sharply, the hunger in his eyes flaring quickly before dying out. 'No, Meghan,' he said softly. 'Don't make that mistake. I haven't changed. The man I was is the man I am. No matter what you think, what I do. No matter.' He squeezed her arm warningly. 'Let's enjoy what we have…and no more.'

Meghan was saved from a reply by another guest crossing to greet them, and the next hour passed in a blur of conversation—

some in Italian, some in English—with Meghan desperately trying to remember the faces and names.

She wouldn't forget the innuendoes.

They laced every sly word, drenched every speculative look.

Hints about his past, his wild days, his many women. She heard the censure, the disapproval, sometimes the reluctant rakish admiration.

Everyone knew who Alessandro had been. Who he was.

Everyone but her.

After an hour she could take no more. She excused herself to the ladies' room, weaving among the guests in search of an escape, no matter how temporary.

'*Buona sera*, Signora di Agnio.'

Stefano Lucrezi lounged in a quiet corner, his wine glass cupped in one palm. He took in her bunched fists and desperate look with one sardonic sweep of his eyes. 'Are you trying to run away?'

'Yes,' Meghan replied, stung to honesty at last. 'These people are piranhas.'

'They scent an easy kill.'

She stopped, stared uncertainly. 'What do you mean?'

Stefano shrugged. 'No one ever expected Alessandro di Agnio to get married.'

'I've gathered that,' she replied, a bit tartly. 'I also understand he's had plenty of women, plenty of parties, and that he's probably been the most notorious playboy Milan—and Italy—have ever seen!'

She'd meant to be sarcastic, but Stefano just nodded slowly. 'Then you are starting to understand.'

Meghan was more shocked by Stefano's admission than she cared to admit, but she rallied her courage and spread her hands wide. 'So what? Lots of men—Italian men—have similar pasts. He's CEO of an important company. He's married now. What matters is *now*.' She so desperately wanted to believe that was true.

'Yes,' Stefano agreed quietly. 'But people don't want to forget. They can't. Alessandro least of all.'

Meghan shook her head, though she'd suspected as much. 'Then what can I do? I don't want the past to destroy us.'

'Has he told you about his brother?'

'He died. That's all I know.'

'Roberto was CEO of the company after their father died. He'd been groomed for the role since infancy, but he was hopeless at it. He was an artist, and he could not make good business decisions. When he died Alessandro took over, but there was not much to work with. People…' Stefano paused, his expression momentarily guarded. 'They doubted he could do it, but he has. He has brought the company back from the brink of ruin. He has proved many, many people wrong, *signora*. I hope he is proved right in you.'

'So do I,' Meghan whispered.

He nodded towards her necklace. 'One of his designs.'

'What?' Meghan touched the necklace, shocked. 'Alessandro designed this?'

'Yes—a hobby of his.' Stefano's face was shadowed for a moment. 'He doesn't like people to know…it's merely a pastime.'

Alessandro was quiet on the way home. Meghan watched him from under her lashes, saw the implacable lines of his face and knew he would not want to talk. He would certainly not want to answer questions.

Yet she had so many.

He needs love.

Did he? Meghan wondered achingly. She so wanted to be able to give it to him…if only he would accept her gift. If only he would dispel his own shadows…or let her help him do it.

'Did you have a good time tonight?' she finally asked, breaking the silence that hung like a pall of gloom over the car.

'No, but I didn't expect to,' Alessandro replied shortly. His eyes slid to Meghan, roamed over her. 'But I did enjoy seeing you in that dress, and picturing what you look like underneath.'

Meghan swallowed, smiled. Sex. That was what he was going to reduce it to now—what he wanted it to be.

She forced herself to smile. Knew she couldn't make him love her. The only power she had now was her love for him. It would have to be enough.

'I'm yours to command.'

Alessandro's eyes lit with a feral pleasure. 'Good.'

He came to her when she was in the bedroom, wiping her make-up off with a tissue.

He stood silently behind her, his hands resting on her shoulders, his face dangerously blank.

'Can you help me with the necklace?' Meghan asked lightly, though she trembled inwardly at the now-familiar mask he wore. A mask she didn't like. Didn't understand.

He obeyed, undoing the intricate clasp. He laid the necklace on the table and then looked at her. Their gazes met in the mirror, his face was still blank except for a cold, predatory smile.

'Take off your clothes.' It came out as a command, blunt and base, and Meghan stiffened, startled, uncertain.

'Take them off, Meghan,' he said silkily. 'I want to look at you.'

She hesitated, hating the cold smile he humiliated her with, yet seeing—wanting to see—desperation in his eyes. He was driven to this, and she didn't understand why.

'Scared?' he mocked softly.

She lifted her chin, met his chilling gaze, and obeyed.

Turning around slowly to face him, she slipped off the dress and it fell in a pool of silk around her feet. She took off her bra and panties and stood there naked, proud, unashamed.

Trembling.

His gaze swept her, raked her, inspecting and assessing.

Why was he doing this? Meghan didn't know. She wouldn't let herself feel the humiliation, the hurt. She'd felt it before, and that life was gone now. For ever. She came to him in love, even if he didn't know it. Even if he wouldn't accept it.

'Touch me.' His bold gaze challenged her, and simply, silently, she moved forward.

She stood before him while he watched her unbutton his shirt. She willed her hands not to shake. Meghan felt his muscles flex under her fingers, knew he was not unaffected by her, even though his still, stony stance made her think otherwise.

Her hands moved lower, hovered at his belt buckle.

'Touch me, Meghan. *Touch me.*' His voice was quiet, lethal, yet she could hear the need, the plea underneath the command. At least, she thought she could.

She hoped.

He was different. *This* was different.

She undid his buckle, slid his trousers down his legs, dropping down to her knees in front of him. He groaned softly, his hands fisted in her hair, pulling her to him.

She kissed him there softly, reverently, and with a shuddering gasp he pulled her up into his arms, burying his head in her hair, breathing in the scent of her as if it were air, as if it would save him.

'Why don't you stop?' he groaned against her hair, her eyes, her mouth. '*Why don't you stop?*'

'Stop?' she repeated uncertainly, accepting his kisses, his regrets.

'Stop loving me.'

Everything inside her stilled, became suspended and motionless. She touched his face with her hands, looked into his eyes, saw the anguish. 'You *know*?' She was shaken by his admission, by hers. By the truth they both knew.

'Don't, Meghan. Don't do it. Stop yourself. For your own sake, for mine, stop.' He was still kissing her, each touch a plea. 'I don't want to hurt you.'

But I will. The words hovered in the air, unspoken. Not needing to be said.

'I can't stop,' Meghan whispered. 'I don't want to.'

He shook his head in denial even as he laid her gently on the bed. 'No. No. You don't know…'

'Tell me.' She arched up, gasping as he touched her, his fingers slipping inside, so knowing, so tender, drawing her fevered response.

'No…Meghan.' His voice was ragged as he entered her warmth, filled her once again. Meghan moved beneath him, accepting his weight, the solid strength of him above and inside her.

He buried his face in her shoulder, his lips on her neck, gasping as they both moved, rocking, wanting, finding…and then shattering into pleasure. 'Meghan…I need you too much.'

Meghan clung to him, stroked his face, his hair. His words echoed in her mind with a flicker of hope.

He needed her. It wasn't love, but it was something.

It was all she had, and she clung to it fiercely.

* * *

Two days later Alessandro came home with two envelopes and a secretive smile.

Meghan was in the lounge, curled up with a book. Since that night of both pain and pleasure they had not talked of love—her love—again. Meghan had not wanted to mention it. She couldn't face the certain rebuff.

Alessandro had reverted—as he always did—into the charming, urbane man she'd once thought was his real self and now knew was not.

Even though she still wanted to find the truth she'd been grateful for the reprieve, a respite from the intensity. They talked, they ate, they made love. Life, on the surface, was simple. It wasn't real. It was a half-life, a life of pleasant pretence.

Meghan wondered how long it would last.

How long they could both keep it up. One of them was certain to break.

Shatter.

Now she took in his teasing, expectant smile with a little fizz of anticipation.

'What is it? What do you have?'

He handed her the first envelope. 'See for yourself.'

Meghan opened it, scanned the embossed paper. It was a letter from one of the American schools in Milan, offering her an interview.

'Alessandro!' she exclaimed. 'How did you arrange…?'

'I had your CV from Stanton Springs faxed to them. It was a matter of minutes.'

'And some ingenuity.'

He shrugged, the movement one of instinctive inherited male arrogance. 'That I have.'

'The interview is next week!' Meghan marvelled. 'I can't believe it!' She glanced at him over the letter, sincerity shining in her eyes. 'Thank you.'

Her gratitude bothered him; she saw it in his dismissive shrug, heard it in his brusque tone. 'It was easy. Open the other one.'

She opened the second envelope. A postcard fell out.

It was a vista of an aquamarine sea, a stunning white sand

beach. Meghan read the place name on the back of the card. 'Amorphos?'

'A Greek island, very small, very secluded. We leave tomorrow morning.'

Her eyes flew to his. 'Tomorrow?'

'I've arranged with my mother to buy the necessary things for you that you don't have already. Your bags are packed. There is nothing keeping us here.'

'Our honeymoon,' Meghan said in dawning delight, and he pulled her into an embrace, gave her a brief, hard kiss.

'Yes…where no one can find us.'

Meghan smiled, but she couldn't keep from thinking, *We can't run for ever.*

They took Alessandro's private jet to Amorphos, so there was just the two of them in the sumptuous interior, feasting on strawberries and chilled champagne.

Meghan glanced out at the Mediterranean below them, a blue blanket stretching to the horizon.

'I can't believe this is real,' she murmured, and Alessandro smiled.

'It's as real as we want it to be.'

She tensed slightly, aware that his remark was cryptic. Nothing so far had been very real.

This trip, just like their life in Milan, was a fantasy as manufactured as the Marmore Falls—a torrent one moment, a trickle the next.

It wouldn't be real until Alessandro confessed, shared the secrets that drove him to despair, that turned him into a desperate stranger.

Until he trusted her…loved her.

When would that happen? How could she make it happen?

Don't think you can save me.

The warning rang in Meghan's mind, echoed through her soul.

But you're worth saving.

She took a sip of champagne, determined to shrug such fears away, for now at least. The bubbles fizzed pleasantly through her.

'So, Di Agnio Enterprises can spare you for a few days?'

'They have to.' Alessandro stretched out in the seat opposite her. 'I am the CEO, after all. I make the rules.'

Meghan twirled her champagne flute in her fingers. 'Stefano mentioned that the company was on the brink of ruin. You saved it.'

Alessandro stilled. 'He exaggerates.'

Meghan felt her heart skip and then beat double-time at Alessandro's cold look, but she pressed on anyway.

'Does he? He seemed quite certain about his facts.'

'He was gossiping like a laundry woman, then,' Alessandro replied shortly. 'It's hardly like him.'

Meghan leaned forward. 'Don't blame him. He was trying to help me.'

'Help *you*?' Contemptuous disbelief delicately laced his words.

'Yes, as a matter of fact,' she replied with some spirit. 'Help me understand you, Alessandro, because you're hell to understand!'

He stared at her, eyes dark and cold as a lake in winter. Meghan held her breath, wondering if she'd pushed him too far. She hadn't meant to start this conversation, hadn't wanted to ask for answers. She just couldn't help herself. She wanted to know so much.

She wanted to understand.

'Maybe I am.' He smiled at her, coldly, and Meghan made herself press on.

'Stefano—he said your brother was an artist, that he didn't have a head for business. No one thought—'

'I know what people did and did not think,' Alessandro cut in shortly. 'And do not think to blame my brother. He did the best he could, and if he made any unwise business decisions it was because he was too naïve, too *trusting*, and people led him astray—' He broke off suddenly, his breathing ragged, and stared out of the window.

Meghan sat back, reeling from the bitterness that had twisted his voice, his features.

'Remember, Meghan, I married you because you don't know me. Don't understand me.' His eyes flashed dangerously. 'And I want to keep it that way.'

'What kind of marriage is that?' Meghan asked, a desperate edge to her voice. 'You can't—'

'The kind we agreed on,' Alessandro cut in with smooth, steely determination. 'Don't think to change it. I warn you, I will not allow it. You may think you love me, but you don't. You don't even know me. If you did—' He stopped, stared out of the window again, his face a mask.

'If I did…?' Meghan prompted softly.

'It hardly matters. Your love is worthless to me.'

The cold, casual dismissal sent stabbing pain through her. She blinked quickly. 'It's not worthless to me.'

'It should be. I warned you, Meghan. Don't forget that.' His mouth was a hard, unforgiving line. He reached forward and poured them both more champagne. 'Now,' he said with silky, lethal intent, 'let's try to enjoy the rest of our *honeymoon*, shall we?'

The rest of the trip passed in miserable silence, Meghan drowning in the fresh sorrow Alessandro had caused.

He did it on purpose. She knew that. He hurt her, drove her away intentionally, to keep her from loving him.

She could only blame herself; she'd known the terms when she'd agreed to the marriage.

It was her own fault now for trying to change them.

She'd just never expected to love so deeply, so purely, so hopelessly.

Was it hopeless? Would Alessandro never learn—perhaps never admit—that he loved her? Was she mad to think he might?

Meghan blinked back tears. The thought of years ahead in a loveless, soulless marriage made her wonder if she could stand it. Yet life without Alessandro at all was not even worth contemplating.

The plane landed on the resort's private airstrip, and Meghan and Alessandro stepped out into the hot, dry sunshine.

She rallied her numbed emotions, smiled at the Grecian paradise stretched out before them for their own pleasure, and said, 'This looks wonderful.'

Alessandro's eyes glinted approval at her change of mood. 'I'm sure we can make it so,' he murmured.

She smiled stiffly, wondered if she had the strength to act the affectionate wife—not loving, never that—when her heart was breaking. Not even breaking. A break would be clean. It was twisting with a torturous pain that Meghan wasn't sure would ever end.

The resort catered to a most exclusive crowd, and Meghan and Alessandro had their own villa, luxurious and intimate.

'Not bad,' Alessandro commented after the porter had left. Meghan took in the combination living and dining room, the tiled floor and simple yet sumptuous furniture, a sliding glass door leading directly to the beach and an aquamarine sea that sparkled like a jewel only metres away.

'Not bad?' she repeated with a little laugh. 'It's paradise.'

'I can hardly wait to enjoy it,' Alessandro murmured, and he moved towards her purposefully.

Meghan tried to return his kiss, tried to fan the flicker of desire in her core. Alessandro began to deftly unbutton her sundress and she stood there silently, her eyes closed, wishing this misery that consumed her heart, her soul, gone.

'Meghan?' Her dress was half off her shoulders when he looked up in perplexity. 'What is it—what is wrong?'

Meghan swallowed, choking down her sorrow. 'Nothing… I'm just tired.'

He paused, his eyes sweeping over her face, guessing at the truth. Meghan blinked, swallowed. Carefully he zipped her dress back up.

'Then you must rest.'

Taking her hand gently, he led her to the bed, tucked her in, and kissed her forehead.

'Rest. There will be plenty of time later.' He smiled softly, his eyes shadowed, and left the room.

Meghan lay in darkness and pressed her face into the pillow, willing the hot rush of tears back. They came anyway.

How could he be so kind, so tender, if he didn't love her? Was it an act? A deceit?

Who was the real Alessandro…? And did *that* man love her?

After a while she fell into an uneasy doze, awoke with her

tears spent. This was her honeymoon. It wasn't the time to demand answers, confessions. She wanted to enjoy it. She wanted Alessandro to enjoy it. The only way to ensure that was to work hard.

Scrubbing her cheeks, Meghan got out of bed.

Over the next week she worked hard to make sure they enjoyed themselves. They chatted rather than talked; joked rather than shared. Meghan kept her voice light. She didn't ask any questions. She wanted Alessandro happy, even if it hurt. She wanted to make him smile, laugh.

She wanted to heal him, but she didn't know how.

They swam and snorkelled, sunbathed and slept. They ate the delicious, plentiful Greek food, and drank the rich red wine. They made love—on the king-sized bed, in the kitchen, in the bath, on the cool white sand as the moon rose above the sea, turning it to silver.

Lying on the bed one evening, listening to the waves lap on the shore and to Alessandro's gentle breathing, Meghan wondered if she would ever be able to expect more. Hope for more.

For something real.

She didn't know how long she could last, how long her heart could last, living this loveless life.

I love him. I want him to love me.

She closed her eyes and sighed, willing herself to be content with what Alessandro offered.

Her only hope was that he would change, that he would come to love and trust her with time. She had nothing else.

On their last night they walked to a taverna in the village and sat outside. Fairylights were twined in the arbour that surrounded the tables, and the water lapped only metres from their feet, fishing boats knocking gently together as the moon cut a silver swath across the calm surface of the sea.

Meghan picked at her souvlaki, wondering what the future held for them, for their marriage. It was easy to pretend on a beautiful island. Real life back in Milan, with all of its shadows and memories, was something different altogether.

Alessandro covered her hand with his own. 'It has to end, *cara*. It always does.'

Meghan wondered if he meant the honeymoon, or something more. Another warning?

She bent her head, let her hair fall to obscure her face. Now was not the time to ask such questions, demand such answers. She knew instinctively Alessandro would recoil. Regret. Repulse.

When would the right time be?

'Alessandro?' They both jerked in surprise at the sensual female voice. A woman stood in front of their table, white-blonde hair framing a sharp, pixie face, her wide blue eyes darting speculatively between Alessandro and Meghan. She was dressed in an extremely skimpy and expensive sundress.

'Emilia.' Alessandro's voice was terse. He stood as a matter of form, of courtesy. 'It has been a while.'

'Hasn't it?' Although she spoke in rapid Italian, this one conversation Meghan was determined to follow. 'This isn't your usual type of place,' she said with a husky laugh. 'Too quiet by far. I came for a bit of rest and relaxation, but I'm already bored.'

'I'm sorry to hear that,' Alessandro replied with wintry politeness.

'Are you?' Her smile curled upwards, as sleek and sly as a cat's. 'Who's your friend?'

Alessandro's eyes narrowed. 'This is my wife—Meghan,' he said coldly. 'We're on our honeymoon.'

'Your *wife*?' Emilia let out a peal of incredulous laughter. 'You're joking! You? Married?'

'I assure you it is true, and a most pleasant truth at that.'

Emilia's gaze raked contemptuously over Meghan. 'This milky miss? Come on, Alessandro. She could amuse you for a day, a week, not much more. I know you...I know your pleasures.' Her smile was so intimate, so suggestive, that Meghan gave a little gasp of wounded surprise.

Alessandro's body was taut, his mouth a thin slash of anger. 'You are insulting me and my wife.'

Emilia's eyes narrowed. 'Her, perhaps,' she agreed, her voice lowered to a hiss. 'But you? That would be hard to do.'

Meghan saw the flash of acknowledgement in his eyes before he bit out, 'I will ask you to leave.'

Her lips tightened, and she turned to Meghan, speaking slowly now for her benefit. 'Forgive my rudeness. Alessandro and I go a long way back. I'd no idea he'd changed so very much.' She glanced back at him slyly. 'If indeed he needed changing.'

'You must have known he'd taken over Di Agnio Enterprises,' Meghan pointed out in what she hoped was a reasonable tone, though she felt like clawing the other woman's eyes out. 'It seems you are not such good friends with my husband as you thought.'

'Perhaps you're right,' Emilia acknowledged with an icy smile. 'I never would have imagined him latching on to a woman like you.' She turned to Alessandro, touched her fingers to her lips and boldly pressed them to Alessandro's mouth. '*Ciao, bello.*'

He stood still, a muscle ticking in his jaw, his eyes both blazing and cold.

Then she left.

Meghan stared down at her virtually untouched souvlaki. The silence stretched between them, thin and taut as a wire, oppressive as a leaden weight.

'I guess she's not too happy you're married,' she finally managed, trying to keep her voice light and amused and failing miserably.

Alessandro's eyes and voice were flat, cold. 'She wouldn't be. Emilia and I used to be lovers.'

Icy shock drenched her, left her near to trembling. It didn't surprise her—of course she'd guessed as much—but it still hurt.

And Alessandro's cold, calculating delivery of such a fact hurt even more.

'Used to be,' she finally repeated, lifting her chin. 'That's what's important now.'

Alessandro's mouth turned up in a mocking smile. 'How fortunate I am to have such an understanding wife,' he remarked lightly. 'And such sensitivity will surely come in useful, considering I'd slept with at least half the women at the cocktail party the other night.'

Meghan's vision blurred, whether from tears or shock she didn't know.

'That doesn't matter,' she whispered, though it felt as if it mattered very much.

'Oh, good,' Alessandro said musingly. 'Because it's probably more like two-thirds.'

'I know you were a playboy, a womaniser, Alessandro,' Meghan said through gritted teeth. 'It doesn't matter now. I know you'll be faithful.'

'Do you?' he mocked, and she gripped the edge of the table, struggling to hold onto her composure, her calm.

She wanted to break down completely.

'Why are you doing this?' she finally asked in a low voice. 'You're deliberately trying to provoke me. To hurt me.'

Alessandro leaned forward, his eyes glittering with malicious intent. 'But *gattina*,' he said softly, 'I'm showing you so you know not to be hurt. This is who I was—who I am. You can't change me. You can't save me.'

Right then Meghan didn't even want to try.

She barely remembered the rest of the meal. She must have eaten and drunk, because their plates were cleared away, her glass refilled. She lived in a shocked daze, wondering why Alessandro hurt her so much, why she let him.

Surely enough was enough?

She couldn't keep doing this.

It wasn't worth it.

But I love him.

Meghan had wanted power for herself this time, had married for it, but she'd become its victim instead. Again.

Alessandro's victim.

The pain of that realisaton sliced her soul in two—was worse than anything she'd known before.

And she didn't know what to do.

They walked back to their villa in silence, the air wrapping them in a warm, sultry blanket, so different from the shattered atmosphere that lay between them like a thousand splinters of hurt emotion, devastated feeling.

Back in the villa, Meghan walked on wooden legs to the bedroom. She undressed, slipped into her nightgown—another silky confection that made nonsense of what was between them now.

She lay still in bed, her eyes hot and dry.

She was past tears.

It was too late for them, anyway.

Alessandro came in after a little while. He peeled off his clothes and slipped between the cool sheets, his back, an expanse of indifference, towards her.

She wouldn't let it end this way tonight, Meghan thought.

She wouldn't be a victim.

She wouldn't run away.

She would take control. She would demand it.

She reached for him, found herself grabbing his shoulders, pulling him over to her. She cupped his face in her hands and kissed him hard, in demand.

A brand.

He didn't respond. She sensed rather than felt his surprise, and after a moment he rolled away from her.

'No, Meghan. Not like this.'

His rejection, on top of everything else, was too much.

She'd had enough.

'*Yes*, like this.' She pushed him onto his back, smiling as his eyes widened in surprise. She straddled him, her thighs pressed against his manhood, her own eyes blazing.

She felt the answering stir of his own desire, saw the flicker of admiration in his eyes as she sat above him, naked and bold.

She had him in her thrall, in her power. He was splayed beneath her, waiting, wanting.

Then Meghan smiled sadly.

'I'm not a whore,' she said softly. 'And I won't use a whore's tricks to bind you to me. I love you. I know you don't love me. You can run away from that, you can try to make me run, but you can't change the truth.'

He looked glorious, his chest bare and smooth and brown, his dark hair rumpled against the white linen pillow. His eyes were dark, fathomless, searching.

Then slowly he reached up, held her face in his hands, and brought her lips down to his.

Surrender.

'Make love to me, Meghan.' He smiled against her mouth, his hips rocking hers. 'Make love to me.'

With a small cry of acceptance, she did, letting him fill her, letting herself be filled to overflowing. Letting the physical joy and pleasure be enough—because right now it was all they had.

It was too much to bear. Alessandro lay on his side and watched Meghan sleep, curled up like a child, next to him.

It hurt too much.

He hadn't asked for her love, hadn't wanted it.

Hadn't ever expected it.

Yet now it was his.

Precious, rare, beautiful.

He rolled on his back and closed his eyes. What could he do with such a gift? He couldn't even begin to know its value, to understand its worth.

He only knew that it was a gift he would lose, utterly, hopelessly, when she discovered the truth.

Had he actually imagined that he could keep it from her? That the denizens of Milan, eager for his blood, his shame, would keep it from her? The few comments she'd heard so far, the innuendoes she'd figured out, were nothing, *nothing*, to the secrets that remained.

And when she discovered them he knew he'd see disgust instead of tenderness, revulsion instead of compassion. Then she would leave. Even if she didn't, even if some brand of honour kept her from going, she would leave in the ways that mattered.

Heart, mind, soul.

He couldn't bear that. It hurt as much as her love did, innocent and ignorant as it was.

So he kept hurting her. He couldn't help it; it was the only way he knew to protect her from more pain. To protect himself.

And he hated himself for it more than ever.

He hated himself more now than when he'd seen his photograph plastered on a thousand tasteless tabloids, than when he'd joked and drunk and slept his way through a worthless life, than when he'd killed his brother.

And he didn't see how it could ever get any better.

CHAPTER ELEVEN

'MAY I come in?'

Emilia Bentano stood at the doorway of the Milan town house, a heavy designer bag over one shoulder.

'I'd rather you didn't,' Meghan managed through stiff lips, after the shock of seeing this woman again—at her door—had eased.

'I know I didn't come off well in Greece,' Emilia said. 'I'm sorry about that.'

'Are you?' Meghan doubted it. So why was the woman here? To sow more discord between her and Alessandro?

That, she thought grimly, could hardly be done. In the week since they'd returned from Amorphos he'd been aloof, removed. The mask firmly in place. It happened every time their bodies—their souls, their hearts—joined, no matter how briefly.

He drew away; he grew cold. His charm was interspersed with careless mocking comments, a calculated indifference meant to drive her away.

Sometimes Meghan wondered if it would be enough to make her go.

She was so tired of the strain, the pretence. She wanted something real and warm and safe.

This was not part of our bargain.

Leaving him would tear her apart, heart and soul, mind and body. She would never be the same again. She would never be whole.

She didn't know what else to do.

This slow torture was accomplishing the same thing, only more slowly, more painfully.

And yet at night Alessandro reached for her. Their bodies merged with a desperate yearning that seemed at odds with the strained pleasantries exchanged each day.

They didn't speak, yet his eyes burned into hers as if memorising her features, as if sending forth a plea.

She just didn't know if she had the strength to believe any more. To fight for it.

'I wanted to talk to you,' Emilia said quietly, sensing Meghan's indecision, offering sincerity. 'I wanted to talk to you about Alessandro…perhaps explain why he is the way he is.'

Meghan's hand tightened on the door handle. A warm breeze caressed her face; she could smell the begonias that tumbled in a riot from their pots onto the steps.

'What do you mean?'

Emilia shrugged, smiled. 'Don't you have questions? Haven't you wondered? Everyone has seen what a transformation Alessandro has made in these last months…wondered if it will last. If it's real.'

'I know it's real,' Meghan said coldly, but her heart was hammering and there was a hollow ring to her words that even she heard.

Emilia raised her eyebrows, cool and knowing. 'Do you? Do you really, Meghan? Because if I were you in your place I'd wonder. I'd wonder very much.'

'But you're not in my place,' Meghan observed with a detachment she was far from feeling. 'As much as you may have once wanted to be.'

Emilia was unfazed. 'Did Alessandro tell you that? Yes, we were lovers. I once thought we might marry… After all, a man like Alessandro would expect to marry eventually, and we're very much alike.'

The thought that Alessandro was similar to this walking piranha made Meghan taste bile in her throat. Alessandro was nothing like this…not the Alessandro she knew.

The man she wanted him to be…the man she thought he wanted to be.

Yet was that really him? Or a façade?

A fake.

'I think,' Meghan said slowly, 'you're just trying to cause trouble. But I know you'll bother me until I let you have your say, so you might as well come in.'

Emilia's mouth curved up into a triumphant smile. Meghan stepped reluctantly aside, and the other woman sashayed into the house with such sultry confidence that Meghan wished she hadn't given in.

Yet she wanted to know.

No matter what the truth meant, what it revealed.

She wanted to know.

Then there would be no more secrets.

'What a quaint little home,' Emilia said with a gurgle of laughter. 'Does Alessandro spend much time here?'

Meghan heard the disbelief in her tone, as if she couldn't imagine Alessandro relaxing in such a boring, bourgeois place.

Maybe he was bored, she thought numbly. Maybe it was all getting too old, too familiar. And it had only been a few weeks.

She led the way into the friendly square lounge, with its squashy red sofas, its long windows spilling sunshine onto the wide pine boards of the floor.

Emilia looked around with an expression of mild distaste, wrinkling her nose as if she were too polite to mention how awful she found it all.

Meghan gritted her teeth. 'Sit down.'

'Thank you.' She perched elegantly on the edge of a sofa, her bag on her lap. She wore, Meghan saw, a tightly fitting red leather jacket and matching skirt, her legs long and bare, her toenails in open sandals painted scarlet.

Meghan sat across from her in an armchair.

'Now, what is it you want to say?'

'Ah, yes. Well…in fact…' Emilia smiled the smile of a sly cat, a cat with a mouse's tail dangling from its sleek jaws, and opened her bag. 'I thought these might tell the tale better than I ever could.' She took out a sheaf of newspaper clippings. Meghan's stomach dipped.

She held out her hand and took them silently, grateful that her hand didn't tremble. She leafed through them, one eyebrow raised, making her uninterest known though her mouth was dry.

Meghan handed them back, heart pounding, for the meaning was obvious enough. The clippings were plastered with photographs of Alessandro at parties, his arms around various scantily clad women, his expression somewhere between a rake's smile and a drunken leer.

He looked, Meghan thought with a sinking feeling, like someone she never wanted to know.

Emilia smiled and said sweetly, 'Look at this one.' She took the clippings, sifting through them until she came to the one she wanted and handed it back to Meghan, tapping the photo with one scarlet nail.

Meghan glanced down, recoiled slightly from the photograph of a smoking ruin of a car left on the side of the motorway. The one word in big block letters stood out in bold relief: OMICIDIO?

Murder.

She stared unseeingly, unthinkingly, down at the newspaper. She heard Emilia purr, 'Now do you want to know?'

'I think,' Meghan replied, barely keeping her voice above a whisper, 'that you're going to tell me.' She looked up, her eyes still dry, her heart weighing heavy like a stone. 'And then you're going to leave.'

'You know Alessandro was a bit of a playboy?' Emilia began, clearly relishing the telling.

'More than a bit, I believe,' Meghan replied, and Emilia looked slightly discomfited that she took this news so calmly.

'Did you know, then,' she continued in a harder voice, 'that he and his brother were involved in a car accident? A highly suspicious one, with Alessandro as the driver.'

'Suspicious?' Meghan repeated, trying to sound scornful and not quite succeeding. 'What's suspicious about a car accident?'

'A lot of things. They'd just had a very public argument—at one of Milan's fashionable parties. Alessandro was angry, and accused Roberto of something—no one heard exactly what this was, and no one would have believed him anyway, of course. Roberto was loved by everyone—kind, gentle, always turning a blind eye to Alessandro's antics. But this time he got upset. I was there and I saw it.' She leaned forward, eyes glittering, involved now in the story, the drama. Meghan, afraid now, could only watch and listen.

'Roberto looked terrible,' Emilia recalled. 'Pale, shaken, like he was going to be sick. Alessandro kept on at him, accusing him, so Roberto tried to leave. Alessandro wouldn't let him, though—he grabbed his arm and started shouting. They ended up leaving the party together—Alessandro threatening, Roberto looking terrified. The next thing we knew Alessandro had crashed the car, killing his brother while he walked away with barely a scratch.'

Meghan's mind and heart reeled from this information. It could explain so much…if she were able to understand it. Still she shook her head, managed to give a disdainful little laugh. 'Do you honestly expect me to believe that he engineered an accident where his brother was killed and he remained uninjured? That's ludicrous.'

Emilia inclined her head in acknowledgement. 'Perhaps. But the accident was on a stretch of smooth road—not a car in sight, no twists or turns. According to police reports, the car just veered off the road into a tree.'

'It's been known to happen before,' Meghan said.

The bands around her chest, her heart, eased—if only a little. An accident couldn't assign blame, no matter what the newspapers said.

'What did Alessandro say about it?' she asked now. 'He must have given some explanation.'

Emilia shrugged. 'Of course he was driving recklessly. But with the di Agnio name… The car had to have been going seventy miles an hour. It's a miracle he wasn't killed.'

'And the press twisted this into a case of murder?' Meghan shook her head.

'You have to admit it makes a certain amount of sense,' Emilia persisted in a silky purr. 'Think what Alessandro stood to gain from his brother's death—CEO of one of Italy's most important companies, prestige, respect…'

'Oh, has he got those?' Meghan queried sharply. 'Because it doesn't seem to me he has.'

Emilia was silent for a moment, watching Meghan with a sneering pity. 'You have no idea what he was like, do you? He may seem like a handsome knight in shining armour now, all set to rescue you, but in this country he was reviled. Pictures of him have been smeared across the tabloids for years, and I know from experience that rumours about him tend to be true.' Her mouth curved in a lasciviously knowing smile that made Meghan bite down on her lip, taste the metallic tang of blood. 'The public turned a blind eye to all his playboy antics, his women, but they couldn't stand what he did to his brother. They blamed him. They *wanted* to blame him. He destroyed the beloved Roberto di Agnio, Italy's golden boy.'

'I'm sure the press had a field-day with it,' Meghan said tightly, her control beginning to splinter. 'It still doesn't make it his fault.'

'Unless,' Emilia said, her voice little more than a whisper, a hiss, 'he *did* mean to crash the car…'

Meghan felt the blood drain from her face, her body turning icy and numb. Lifeless.

'He had nothing to lose,' Emilia continued with dangerous softness. 'He was a rake, a reprobate, his family had practically disowned him for the things he'd done, the shame he'd brought to them. In a moment of violent jealousy…' She shrugged delicately. 'Who knows what could have happened?'

Meghan sank unsteadily into a chair. Could Alessandro have been so desperate, so unhappy, so *murderous*, he'd tried to kill both himself and his brother?

Could he have been so vile?

'I want you to go,' she said in a thin voice. 'Now.'

Emilia chuckled softly. 'I've given you enough to think about, have I? Good. At least now you know what he's capable of. Alessandro was a desperate, dangerous man, Meghan. He still is. I'll leave the clippings here…just in case you want to look through them again. *Ciao.*'

The front door clicked softly shut behind her.

Meghan let out a shuddering breath and glanced down at the newspaper photograph of the smoking ruin of a convertible. He didn't drive those any more. *Now she knew why.*

She picked up the sheaf of clippings with numb fingers, a numb heart. She sifted through them, steeled herself against the images, glaring, garish, painful.

Alessandro with his arms wrapped around a blonde who was poured into a dress. Alessandro kissing another woman, one eye on the camera, giving a lascivious wink. Alessandro with a woman on each arm and a sardonic smile twisting his features, making him someone she could hate.

It was horrible.

It was wrong.

It was the truth.

She stared at the photographs until her eyes were gritty, forcing herself not to close them against the onslaught of images, realisations, shattered dreams.

This was Alessandro. This was the man he had been, the man he insisted he still was. As much as she'd suspected and feared what he'd done, this was worse. This was so much worse.

She believed he'd changed, but could a man actually change that much?

Was Alessandro even *trying* to change?

Her heart cried *yes*, he was; her mind ruthlessly reminded her of every cruel thing he'd said, every harsh warning he'd given.

He'd *told* her not to trust him, not to love him. He'd told her not to try to understand, to know.

Now she knew, and her ignorance—and innocence—were gone for ever.

How could he be at times so tender, so kind, so understanding, so *loving*? her heart cried out, and her mind replied dispassionately, *You always knew men abused power.*

Meghan stared at the photograph of the car, half-wrapped around a tree on a deserted road. It was charred, a wreck of a car, wrecking a life.

Two lives.

Three.

What had happened that night? Could Emilia possibly be right?

Meghan desperately wanted to believe she couldn't be, yet doubt had created a treacherous crack in her heart she couldn't ignore.

She was faced with the bleak reality that despite what her heart said her mind told her the truth.

She didn't *know* what kind of man Alessandro was.

She couldn't fathom what he was capable of.

So intent was Meghan on the clippings that she didn't register the click of the front door, the sound of soft footsteps. She didn't even notice the shadow that fell over her as Alessandro came into the room, didn't realise he was there until he spoke, ice coating every word.

'Ah. I see you've discovered my past.'

'Alessandro!' Meghan's stomach plunged with nerves; the clippings fell from her lap onto the floor.

His lips curving in a sardonic smile, Alessandro stooped to pick them up. 'Enjoying yourself?' he asked softly. 'Indulging in some vicarious pleasure? I have Emilia to thank for this, no doubt. Or did you manage to dig these up all on your own?' Menace turned his eyes dangerously indigo, his mouth a hard, thin line.

'It was Emilia,' Meghan whispered.

'Ah. She always liked to cause trouble.'

He riffled through the clippings with an uninterested air. 'Ah, yes. I think I remember this one. She was quite good in bed, if I recall. Daring.'

Meghan closed her eyes.

'And this one… Hmm, memory's a bit fuzzy there. Probably had too much to drink. I often did.'

'Don't do this.' She felt faint, dizzy, sick.

Alessandro glanced at her over the top of the clippings and smiled coolly. 'But why not, Meghan? Isn't this what you want to know? Isn't this why I found you here, staring at these photos?'

'I was trying,' Meghan replied as levelly as she could, 'to find out why you are the way you are.'

'Do not!' His voice came out sharp. 'Do *not* psychoanalyse me. I know who I am. These clippings prove it. And if you fell in love with me, Meghan, then you fell in love with a false image. What you wanted me to be, not what I am.'

It was what her own mind had been telling her, and it hurt. It hurt more than she'd ever thought it would to hear him say it, admit it.

'You were kind to me,' Meghan whispered, her eyes starting to pool with tears. The room, the clippings, Alessandro, were all a blur. 'You told me you would never hurt me.'

'*Da tutti i san*, by now you should've realised that wasn't true!'

Her vision swam; she clutched the arm of her chair like an anchor. 'Are you telling me you lied?'

'I got what I wanted,' Alessandro replied dispassionately. 'You.'

'I don't believe it.' She clung to one last hope that even now he would relent. Change. 'This isn't you.'

'Yes, it is. I warned you, Meghan.'

Alessandro's face was a mask, terrible in its blankness. It was as if the life had drained out of him, and Meghan didn't know if she could get it back. She dragged breath into her lungs. 'What about the car accident?'

He stilled, and for a tense moment Meghan wasn't sure what he would do next. What he was capable of. She stiffened, forced herself to remain still.

'Are you asking me if I killed my brother?' he asked, his voice indifferent. 'You saw the headlines. *Omicidio. Assassino.* They speak the truth.'

'It was an accident.'

'Was it?' He raised his eyebrows. 'I read the tabloid gossip, every word. Maybe I picked that stretch of road—crashed the car in a way that would only injure the passenger. Who knows?' He smiled mockingly, and Meghan shook her head, desperate now.

'Alessandro, that can't be true. Even if you were capable of such a thing, it would be an insane risk.'

He walked up to her, tilted her chin with cool fingers so Meghan was looking with anguish into his own blank eyes.

'But don't you know by now that I like to take risks? It's what makes me good at business. You were a risk, weren't you, *gattina*? Too bad that one hasn't worked out.'

She shook her head. 'No, it can't...' Her voice trailed off into desperate silence.

His fingers tightened on her chin. 'Tell me, Meghan,' he said softly, 'when you look at those clippings, what do you feel, think? What do you believe?'

Her mind spun, whirred hopelessly like a stalled engine. She thought of what she'd felt: the horror, the repulsion, the fear, and knew they were reflected in her eyes, her face. She tried to think of a word, an explanation, but nothing came out.

Something flickered to life in Alessandro's eyes and then deadened. Like ash, dust, ice. 'You see?' he said softly. 'You do believe it, don't you? I warned you before. I won't change.' He paused, his voice turning ragged. 'I can't.'

She stared. Her mind blanked. She couldn't speak.

He dropped his hand from her face and glanced down at the clippings; the photograph of the ruined car was on top. 'Damned by silence,' he mocked.

'Alessandro, don't…' she began, her voice a thread, but he ignored her.

'Never mind. It's just as well, you know. I was starting to get bored.'

'Bored?' she repeated faintly, and he smiled, a bitter twisting of his lips.

'Surely you saw in those papers that I'm a man of many tastes, pleasures? I'll get a few things,' he continued tonelessly, 'and move to my flat. You can continue to live here. I don't mind.'

Meghan felt as if she were plummeting through a cold, dark tunnel. She gazed at him in shock, her mind finally catching up, making sense of what was happening. 'What are you saying?'

'I'm saying,' Alessandro replied in clear, cutting tones, 'that I don't want to live with you any more. This marriage was a mistake, a bad risk, but unfortunately neither of us can undo it now. I won't bring shame to the di Agnio name again.' He held up one hand to still the wave of protests rising within her, unspoken. 'You'll still get what you want. I'll come with you to that godforsaken town in Iowa you once called home. I'll give you security. You, on the other hand, need give me nothing.'

'Alessandro…' Meghan was on her knees on the chair, tears streaking silently down her face. She felt as if her world had been torn apart in a matter of minutes and lay around her in bloody shreds. And she hadn't lifted a finger to stop it. She hadn't had the strength. 'This isn't what I want.'

He looked at her as if he didn't care. As if he'd already moved on, forgotten. 'Pity,' he remarked, 'because this is what you're going to get.'

Meghan remained half kneeling on the chair as Alessandro moved through the house. She knew he was gathering his things, preparing to leave her for ever.

And she didn't know what to do.

She hadn't expected this utter rejection—the man she loved turned into a stranger she couldn't even understand.

She should have spoken sooner—done something, thought something, acted. Shown him... But what? She'd still been reeling with shock, with disappointment, with sorrow.

And now it was too late.

It's never too late, her heart cried out, and Meghan forced herself to listen. Alessandro was her second chance at life, at love; she was his. She wouldn't let go of it lightly.

She couldn't let him leave.

Not like this. Never like this.

On weak, wobbling legs she walked up the stairs, her mind buzzing but blank. She wished she knew what to say, what to *think*. She only knew she had to act.

She turned the corner, came to the bedroom door. And saw him.

Alessandro sat on the bed, his head bowed, his hands fisted in his hair. Meghan's heart contracted, ached with a desperate longing that nearly made her stagger.

She recognised that stance, the bleak despair in every agonised line of his body. She'd felt it herself.

It was the look of a person who believed his own soul was damned because everyone had told him it was, even when his heart had cried out for belief, for love.

For salvation.

She'd felt it when one man had condemned her; Alessandro had suffered the judgement of an entire country.

This is the man I love.

This was the man. No matter what he'd thought, what he'd felt, what he'd done.

She loved Alessandro.

And she knew, had to believe, that he was the man she thought he was, knew he was.

The man he meant to be.

She must have made some sound, for he looked up, his face hardening into a mask once more.

'I'll be out of here in a few minutes,' he said coldly. 'Can't you wait?'

'No, I can't,' Meghan said. Her voice was a scratchy breath of sound but she forced it to come out stronger. 'And you won't.'

'I won't?' he repeated in a mocking tone. 'You should know by now there's little I *won't* do, *gattina*.' He stood up, grabbed the half-filled bag at his feet and slung it over one shoulder.

Meghan stood in the doorway, her arms flung out, blocking him. Alessandro walked towards her, one eyebrow raised in incredulous disdain.

'Get out of my way, Meghan.' He spoke softly, quietly, yet she still knew it was a threat.

'No.'

He paused, his eyes sweeping, assessing her, burning her, just as they had when he'd looked at her that first time in the restaurant.

Even then her body, her *heart*, had known this was the man— the man she needed.

And she wasn't going to let him walk away now.

'Haven't you had enough, Meghan? Or did you lose all of your self-respect when that man abused you?' He shook his head. 'Save us the shame of such a scene and let me walk out of here with head held high.'

'I don't think anyone's head is high right now,' Meghan replied in a low voice. 'Yours wasn't a moment ago, and mine isn't now. I'm ashamed—' her breath hitched '—that I didn't answer you downstairs. That I didn't tell you I believed.'

'But you did believe. You believed the truth. Now, enough of this!' His hand slashed through the air. 'Leave me alone. Let me go.'

Meghan's throat ached with unshed tears. She held them back, forced herself to be strong, if only for a moment. Trembling, she put one hand flat on Alessandro's chest, felt his sucked-in breath at the contact. The caress. 'But I can't let you go, Alessandro. I love you.'

He shrugged, determinedly unmoved. 'You love the man I pretended to be to make you marry me.'

'Why would you do that? You didn't have to marry me. I told you that myself. It could have been an affair.'

'You hold yourself rather cheaply,' he said coldly, his mouth twisting.

Meghan's eyes blazed for a second. She might be dying inside—her dreams, her hopes, her heart, all on their last breath, their last chance—but she was still going to fight. Fight for her own shattered hopes, for Alessandro's.

'*You* hold yourself cheaply, it seems,' she responded levelly. 'I don't know your secrets, Alessandro. I don't know all the things you did. I don't want to. But I know—*I know*—that you've been trying to overcome your past. To not be the man the tabloids painted you—the man you and everyone else believed you to be. I've seen you struggle with it. I've seen you lose, and I've seen you win. It's not an act.' Her voice broke into fragments of pain and sorrow, of hope too painful to bear, too precious to lose. 'I believe in you. I love you.'

Alessandro was silent, still. She could feel the energy thrumming through him, a raw, angry pulse.

'It doesn't matter. It's not real.'

'It *is* real,' Meghan flashed. 'You can't keep denying what I know! I don't care what you do, how many times you try to push me away. I know who you are and I love you!'

'No, you don't!' His voice came out in a savage roar, ripped from his body, his lungs, and Meghan jerked back, startled. His face twisted into a grimacing sneer as he dropped his bag on the floor, grabbed her arms. 'What do you want from me? What do I have to do to show you I'm not the man you think I am?' His fingers dug into her arms and Meghan forced herself to submit, to stare into his face, a beautiful face no longer blank, but tormented by pain and misery.

He felt. The mask had dropped, and she was glad.

'There's nothing you can do,' she said quietly. Her voice

shook only a little. 'You've already shown me, Alessandro. You've shown me with compassion, love and tenderness what kind of man you are. The man I love.'

He let out a low, rasping sound; Meghan thought it was a laugh. Then he pulled her to him, her breasts flattening against his chest, and kissed her with a hard desperation that felt like a bruise.

Meghan's hands crept up his chest, wound around his neck. She pulled him closer and gentled the kiss, turning it into something loving and warm.

He refused, breaking it off, coming up for air with a choked laugh of disbelief. 'Have you no self-respect?' he demanded, and though pain was slicing cleanly through her, Meghan answered steadily.

'I didn't. But you gave it back to me. You can't take it away again.'

'Can't I?' he jeered, and, pulling on her wrists, led her to the bed, tossing her carelessly down on it. Meghan lay there, her heart pounding so loudly it seemed to fill the room with its desperate beat. She was on her back, splayed, helpless.

She thought of the first time he'd touched her, what he'd said. *I'm not going to touch you. I'm not that kind of man.*

No, he wasn't. She still believed. Even now, when he was determined to show her differently, to prove her love was worthless.

Especially now.

The final test.

He looked down at her, his hands on his hips, his expression coldly mocking. 'Scared, Meghan?'

'No.' Her voice wavered, but she kept looking at him. Forced herself to meet the icy steel of his eyes.

'You should be.'

'What are you going to do, Alessandro? Try to make me stop loving you? Is that what this is about?'

'What this is about?' he mused, his smile a taunt. He dropped his hand down to her ankle, ran it slowly, temptingly up her bare leg—a deliberate, calculated caress. Meghan didn't move even when his hand travelled further upwards, under her skirt, teased her at the joining of her thighs, his eyes still on hers, still cold.

Even now she felt the flickerings of desire, unbearably sweet, piercing the anger.

'Do you want me,' he said in disbelief, 'even now?'

Unashamed, Meghan raised her head, looked at him. Offered herself to him. 'Yes. I love you.'

He jerked back his hand, scalded by her honesty. 'This isn't about love!'

'Yes, it is. I love you. And you love me.' She met his gaze, let her eyes blaze into his.

He shook his head, hunched his shoulders. After a moment of tense silence, he said, 'Meghan, I've never wanted to hurt you.'

'Then don't.'

'*You don't know me!*' He bit the words out, raking a frustrated hand through his hair.

'I don't know who you were,' Meghan corrected. 'But I know you now.'

He shook his head, his eyes blanking again. The mask was slipping down once more, and Meghan knew she couldn't let it return.

'Alessandro, don't.' She struggled up from the bed, pulled her skirt back down. 'Don't shut me out.' She stood before him, begging. 'What will it take to prove to you that you can't turn me away? That I won't desert you?'

'You've proved that to me, Meghan,' he snapped savagely. 'You're like a little beaten dog, accepting every careless kick. I can't *get* you to leave!'

Meghan blinked. She wanted to be strong. She *wanted* to be able to do this. She just didn't know if she had the strength.

'I was honest with you,' she said, after a long, taut moment, her voice barely audible. 'I told you my secrets. My shadows. I took the risk.'

'What risk?'

'The risk of having you not believe me. Of having you disgusted by me, by my past. Believing of me what Stephen did. It was a big risk.'

He was silent, arrested, his eyes narrowed. Meghan dragged a breath into her lungs, willed herself to continue.

'You told me you liked taking risks. *I* was a risk, you said. Well, sorry, Alessandro, but I don't see that from here. All I see is a man haunted by his past. A man afraid to tell the truth. A coward.'

'I am *not* a coward!' His eyes flashed flint and his hands balled into fists. Meghan lifted her chin.

'No? Then tell me the truth.'

'I told you the truth.'

'You told me the tabloid truth. I want to know what really happened the night of the car accident.'

'That has nothing—'

'Yes, it does,' she cut him off. She pressed her hands flat against his chest. He shrugged away, but she kept on holding him. Touching him. 'I think I'm smart enough to realise that even being the world's biggest playboy wouldn't drive you like this. Torture you like this. It has to be something else. So what else is there? It must be the car accident. Something happened that night—something that is consuming you with guilt. I know what guilt feels like, Alessandro. I know what it *tastes* like. It tastes like cold metal. It rides you, wakes you up in the night, drenched in sweat, in icy terror. *I know*. You said I had shadows, but you have them too, and I don't want them here any more.'

He looked down at her, curled his fingers around her hands as if to remove them, then stopped. His eyes weren't blank; they were shadowed with pain, darkened with sorrow.

'It's not that simple.'

Meghan felt the first tremulous thrill of victory. She leaned in, kissed the rapid pulse of his throat. 'It is.'

Alessandro shook his head, the barest of movements, his eyes closed, his face working into hard lines, harsh angles.

'What happened that night?' Meghan asked softly. 'You argued—you said something to Roberto and he didn't like it. He was shaken, frightened. What did you tell him?'

Alessandro was silent for a long moment. Meghan could hear the ragged rasp of their breathing; the pounding of their hearts. Outside a child laughed, a muted sound of joy from another world.

'I told him the truth.' Alessandro spoke through stiff lips, his eyes focused on a distant place, a remembered time. His voice was little more than a whisper.

'What was the truth?'

His hands curled tightly around hers; he was holding onto her now, Meghan realised. He didn't want her to let go.

She wouldn't. She never would.

'He'd made a mistake.' Alessandro stopped, and Meghan held her breath. She knew it would take time, and it would take pain, to bring the truth from him. She could wait. 'He had no head for business, Roberto,' he continued after a moment, his voice turning toneless. Meghan understood the need to distance himself from the telling. 'He was an artist, burdened by my parents' expectations. He never should have…' He let out a low breath, shook his head, then continued. 'After my father died, the company was Roberto's alone. He made all the decisions, and he couldn't handle the responsibility. He never should have been given it.'

It should have been you, Meghan thought. Alessandro was the one with the head for business; he'd designed the most stunning piece of jewellery she'd ever seen. Yet he'd been passed over since he was a child—perhaps a bit too high-spirited, his mischievous pranks turning wilder as he was continually overlooked. It was so easy to imagine. To understand.

'He made some bad business deals,' Alessandro finally said. 'Ran into debt, terrible debt, and he couldn't get out. He became desperate, but he was also stupid. He wanted to pay back the loan sharks without anyone noticing, so he started embezzling from the company. Our company.'

He looked down at her, regret etched on every line of his face. 'I found out. I wish I hadn't. Roberto would be alive today…'

Meghan doubted that, but she held her tongue. Alessandro's honesty—his confession—was too precious.

'I used to check the company's finances,' he explained, expressionless once more. 'I…I always had an interest. When I realised what was going on I was angry.' He closed his eyes briefly. 'I was very angry—unreasonably so, perhaps—and I went to find him immediately. He was at a party—Paula, his wife, was there. *Everyone* was there. I spoke to him—I tried to keep it private…' Now his voice turned urgent, almost pleading. 'But Roberto decided to brazen it out. He said he didn't know what I was talking about, asked why I was checking up on him, so I stated figures. Facts. Then the life drained out of him. I saw him then, defeated, hopeless, and I was glad.' He looked at her, his face twisted with torment. 'What sort of man does that make me, to feel that way towards my own brother? My own brother, who never did me a moment's harm?'

Meghan shrugged. She felt eerily calm. In control. At last. 'A natural one, to have such a reaction in the heat of the moment.'

'He left the party; I followed him.' He was determined to finish it now, to have the reckoning. 'We got in the car. Once we were alone Roberto became furious. I'd never seen him so angry, so…hateful. I knew he was afraid, but I didn't let him off. I didn't give him any mercy.'

'Did he ask for it?' Meghan asked.

'He told me that I should turn a blind eye to his doings, that he'd always turned a blind eye to mine. I said… I said…' Alessandro dragged in a shuddering breath. 'I said I'd see him rot in hell first.'

Meghan's fingers ached from where he was clenching them, clinging to her as his last hope for redemption. She held on.

'And then?'

'And then…' He drew in another breath. 'And then he said that's just what I'd do.'

Alessandro was silent, his lips pressed tightly together, unable to say any more. To finish the story.

Realisation dawned slowly, achingly. 'He was driving the car, wasn't he?' Meghan said softly. 'He tried to kill you both.'

Alessandro didn't answer. Couldn't. Tenderly Meghan reached up and stroked his face, let her fingers trail along his cheek.

'You took the blame,' she surmised. It all made sense now. It was all so horrifyingly clear. 'You didn't want to sully his perfect reputation, did you? His wife… Your mother…'

'He tried—'

'What did you do? Trade places in the car? Emilia said you walked away without a scratch, but you must have had some injuries.'

'A concussion,' Alessandro said tonelessly. 'I dragged him across to the passenger seat, managed to get myself behind the wheel before I blacked out. It was the only way,' he told her, urgency roughening his tone into a demand. 'Roberto was the kindest, gentlest person... He had a moment of terrible weakness, but one that would be remembered for ever. I knew they'd believe I was driving the car—maybe they'd even think I meant to do it. They'd believe anything of me. It hardly mattered. But Roberto never hurt anyone.'

Except you, she thought. *He hurt you.*

Meghan shook her head slowly; love swelled within her, hurting her with its beauty and joy. *This* was the man she loved. 'And for this you feel guilt? Shame?'

'I killed him,' Alessandro whispered. 'If I hadn't confronted him...if I hadn't said that...' His voice turned angry, savage in its recrimination. 'I knew he was weak. That he didn't have a head for business. I'd always known it. It didn't help matters that I was partying every night, acting the playboy to thumb my nose at my parents and the world. I was stupid and reckless, and no more so than the night I got into that car. If only *I'd* taken the keys...'

'He would have done it another day,' Meghan said calmly. 'Another way. He was desperate, Alessandro, forced into a corner. It's not your fault.'

'It is.' He spoke with such certainty that her heart plummeted; then she felt angry.

'You can't be responsible for someone else's actions! Didn't you show me that when I told you what happened to me? Was I responsible for Stephen's actions? For what he did to me?'

His face twisted in horror. 'Meghan, don't.'

'No—*you* don't,' Meghan snapped back. He looked startled, and she almost smiled. 'I see who you really are. The world even sees it—sees what you've done with Di Agnio Enterprises. Alessandro, you must forgive yourself. If not for your own sake, then for mine.' She paused, her voice turning into an ache as she repeated the words he'd once said to her, the words with which he'd healed her. 'I know, and I accept you. I believe you.' She

paused, tears filling her eyes as her fingers skimmed his cheek.
'I love you.'

Alessandro was silent; his eyes were closed. Meghan's heart
beat a steady, desperate staccato as she wondered what was going
on in his tormented mind, what would happen now.

Then a single tear slipped down his cheek; it dampened her
fingers. Alessandro's grief for his brother. Meghan's breath
caught in her chest; her heart expanded and she could breathe
again. She could believe again.

Alessandro opened his eyes. 'I love you.'

Meghan felt weak with relief, giddy with joy.

He shook his head, took her tear-dampened fingers and lifted
them to his lips. 'I don't know why I have been so blessed to
have a woman who believes in me enough to see me through this.
To make me go through this.' He smiled, the sorrow sifting from
his eyes, revealing a flicker of hope. 'You saved me, Meghan.
You saved me.'

'And you saved me.'

'I need to ask you to forgive me,' he continued in a low voice,
'for hurting you so very much. I did it to drive you away. I
thought it would be easier for both of us. Or at least for me. I
couldn't bear seeing you walk away from me, *gattina.* Seeing you
disgusted by who I was, by who I am.'

'No,' Meghan whispered, 'never that. I know who you are,
Alessandro, and you are the man I love.'

He nodded in acceptance, in wonder. 'You knew even
before I did. How can you know me so well when I was blind
to myself?'

'We were both blind,' she said with a little laugh. 'And we
needed each other to be healed. Forgiven.' *Loved.*

He pulled her towards him, kissed her with a gentle passion
that had her swaying into him completely, surrendering everything. Her heart, her soul, her mind, her body. His. All his.

'I am a blessed, blessed man,' he said, and there was a ragged
edge of incredulous gratitude in his voice.

'No more blessed than I am.'

He nodded, kissing her again, and as sunlight slanted through the windows, sifting patterns on the floor, Meghan realised the shadows were gone. All of them.

All that was left was her and Alessandro, and joy.

Only joy.

QUEENS *of* R♥MANCE

The world's favorite romance writers

New and original novels you'll treasure forever from internationally bestselling Presents authors, such as:

Lynne Graham
Lucy Monroe
Penny Jordan
Miranda Lee

and many more.

Don't miss

THE GUARDIAN'S FORBIDDEN MISTRESS
by Miranda Lee

Book #2701

Look out for more titles from your favorite Queens of Romance, coming soon!

www.eHarlequin.com

HP12701

REQUEST YOUR FREE BOOKS!

2 FREE NOVELS PLUS 2
FREE GIFTS!

YES! Please send me 2 FREE Harlequin Presents® novels and my 2 FREE gifts. After receiving them, if I don't wish to receive any more books, I can return the shipping statement marked "cancel." If I don't cancel, I will receive 6 brand-new novels every month and be billed just $3.80 per book in the U.S., or $4.47 per book in Canada, plus 25¢ shipping and handling per book and applicable taxes, if any*. That's a savings of close to 15% off the cover price! I understand that accepting the 2 free books and gifts places me under no obligation to buy anything. I can always return a shipment and cancel at any time. Even if I never buy another book from Harlequin, the two free books and gifts are mine to keep forever.

106 HDN EEXK 306 HDN EEXV

Name	(PLEASE PRINT)	
Address		Apt. #
City	State/Prov.	Zip/Postal Code

Signature (if under 18, a parent or guardian must sign)

Mail to the **Harlequin Reader Service®:**
IN U.S.A.: P.O. Box 1867, Buffalo, NY 14240-1867
IN CANADA: P.O. Box 609, Fort Erie, Ontario L2A 5X3

Not valid to current Harlequin Presents subscribers.

Want to try two free books from another line?
Call 1-800-873-8635 or visit www.morefreebooks.com.

* Terms and prices subject to change without notice. NY residents add applicable sales tax. Canadian residents will be charged applicable provincial taxes and GST. This offer is limited to one order per household. All orders subject to approval. Credit or debit balances in a customer's account(s) may be offset by any other outstanding balance owed by or to the customer. Please allow 4 to 6 weeks for delivery.

Your Privacy: Harlequin is committed to protecting your privacy. Our Privacy Policy is available online at www.eHarlequin.com or upon request from the Reader Service. From time to time we make our lists of customers available to reputable firms who may have a product or service of interest to you. If you would prefer we not share your name and address, please check here. ☐

HP07